SECOND TIME AROUND

Widowed single parent Elise Trent thought no one could replace her husband Peter, until she met policeman Mark Hampson. She is forced to seriously re-think her life when her mother-in-law Joan accepts a proposal of marriage from long time companion Seth Baxter, and her student daughter Angie and Mark's son Kyle get involved with an action group. Then Elise and Mark are further thrown together by a spate of country house burglaries . . .

MS

MARGARET MOUNSDON

SECOND TIME AROUND

Complete and Unabridged

LINFORD
Leicester

First published in Great Britain in 2012

First Linford Edition
published 2012

British Library CIP Data

Mounsdon, Margaret.
    Second time around. - -
    (Linford romance library)
    1. Love stories.
    2. Large type books.
    I. Title II. Series
    823.9′2–dc23

    ISBN 978–1–4448–1361–6

Published by
F. A. Thorpe (Publishing)
Anstey, Leicestershire

Set by Words & Graphics Ltd.
Anstey, Leicestershire
Printed and bound in Great Britain by
T. J. International Ltd., Padstow, Cornwall

This book is printed on acid-free paper

1

Mark's open face was full of the disappointment he could not hide and he stopped in his tracks as they walked along the lane together. 'Your answer is no?'

'It has to be,' Elise replied, her heart sinking, ' . . . for the moment,' she attempted to soften the blow. Why hadn't she seen this coming?

'May I know why?'

'It's not easy to explain . . . ' Mark's question caught Elise unprepared. There were so many reasons but she so did not want to hurt his feelings.

'Try,' Mark urged as he resumed their walk.

'I want us still to be friends, please?' Elise's gentle French accent was always more pronounced when she was under stress. 'I like you very much.'

'But not enough to want to marry me.'

'It's not that . . . I'm not ready for commitment.'

'Is it because of Angie?'

'You know it isn't.'

'Joan then.'

'No,' Elise insisted, 'and before you ask it's nothing to do with Kyle either. Your son is a marvellous boy and you should be very proud of him.'

'I am,' Mark said and nothing more was said for several long seconds. 'So is it an age thing?' Mark broke the silence that had fallen between them.

'I don't understand.' Elise frowned and slowed her pace.

'You're nearly forty. Is it some sort of early mid-life crisis?'

Elise was a beautiful woman. She had been barely twenty-two when her daughter was born and people often mistook them for sisters, even though she had chestnut hair and her daughter's blonde locks took after her father.

'Certainly not. It's so difficult to explain.'

'I know the hours I work can be

erratic but it's never been a problem between us before, has it?'

'It's not that either.'

'What is it then? I've exhausted all possibilities.'

Elise paused and then sighed before telling him, 'I suppose by marrying you I would feel I was betraying Peter's memory . . . '

Mark sighed. 'Believe me I have every respect for your late husband's memory, Elise, but isn't it time to move on?'

Elise linked her hand through Mark's as they walked up the country lane, past the cricket pitch and through the five barred gate that led to the farm shop run by Joan Trent, Elise's mother-in-law, and where Elise and her daughter Angie lived in a small flat above the premises. An owl hooted in the beech trees and a rabbit bounded through the night grass, his scut creating a flash of white in the darkness.

'Why can't things stay as they are?' Elise asked.

'After eighteen months together I thought it was the right time to develop our friendship into something deeper.'

'Are you saying you no longer wish to be my friend?' Elise asked in consternation.

'That's not what I'm saying at all.' Mark kicked out at a stone. 'We get on well together, our children like each other and go to the same college, even your late husband's mother likes me and we are both free to marry.'

'Put like that you are making me sound unreasonable.'

'I don't want to force you into anything,' Mark's voice was quiet. 'Obviously I misunderstood the situation.'

'If you feel our relationship cannot continue as it is then of course I'll understand, but I have to be honest with you Mark and I feel accepting your proposal would be the wrong thing for me to do at this time. I have too much regard for your feelings to pretend otherwise.'

4

'Thank you for that at least,' Mark replied as they approached the farm shop. 'I appreciate your honesty.'

'Are we still friends?' Elise asked.

'Still friends,' he nodded. 'I won't come in for coffee,' he said as Elise began searching for her key, 'I've a busy day tomorrow. I'll give you a ring some time.'

He kissed Elise on the cheek then waited for her to unlock her door. Once he was sure she was safely inside he turned and made his way back down the lane.

Elise stood on the other side of the door for a few moments catching her breath, listening to Mark's receding footsteps. Had she done the right thing? Mark was a good man and she liked him very much, but did she love him? At the age of thirty-nine was it reasonable to expect the heart-stopping emotional roller coaster she had experienced the first time she'd seen Peter? She didn't know. All she knew was she wasn't ready for marriage again. With a sigh, she locked the door before heading upstairs.

*   *   *

'Anybody in?' The bell rang in the shop.

Glad to have an excuse to abandon her paperwork, Joan Trent bustled through from the back office. A sensibly clad woman was waiting by the till.

'Good morning. What can I do for you?' Joan said politely.

'Holly Hock House,' the woman introduced herself. 'We've come to do the nature trail.'

'Of course.' Joan smiled. 'It's all ready.'

Outside Joan could hear a party of schoolchildren squealing with laughter. She guessed that Gertie was probably up to her usual tricks. Those in the know knew better than to leave their possessions unattended when Gertie the goat was around. She was a sweet animal but no respecter of personal belongings and would happily chomp her way through anything available.

'The trail normally takes about an hour to complete,' Joan explained as she passed over pencils and a pre-printed list of questions for the children to complete. 'Follow the green arrows and you won't get lost.'

The group assembled by the departure point and the teacher distributed the questionnaires to eager little hands. The answers to Joan's questions were easy to spot and the children always had a lot of fun playing detective and following her clues.

'I'll see you in about an hour.' Joan waved them off. 'If you've any problems I'll be in the shop.'

The outings ended up with refreshments and a question and answer session in her kitchen. Parents were encouraged to join the parties and Joan would note with satisfaction that not many of them left her farm shop without purchasing something. Her shelves groaned with the local produce she liked to support and her newly introduced gift wrapping service for the honey and home-made jams and jellies was proving a popular attraction.

The decision to diversify had been her late husband's.

'We've had two lean years,' he'd explained after a challenging meeting with their accountants. 'If we're to survive we need to branch out. Now our USP — unique selling point — is Merritt's Wood.'

Their paddock backed onto the wood. It had been designated an area of great natural beauty and over the years many rare plants and endangered species had thrived in the unpolluted surroundings.

Richard consulted an efficient marketing analyst who had instantly taken their proposal on board.

'Your small holding is ideal for nature trails. You would need very little initial outlay and it would put Trents on the map.'

Richard's untimely death two years into the scheme had almost persuaded

Joan to abandon the project and sell up, but her daughter-in-law, Elise, and teenage granddaughter Angie, had been such towers of strength, so with their love and support she had been able to carry on.

Now Joan was glad she had. She loved to listen to the young visitors' excited questions. Many of them were inner city children enjoying their first visit to the country. On one occasion she had difficulty keeping a straight face as she informed an earnest looking little boy that although hens did indeed lay eggs, pigs did not lay sausages.

Some of the shyer children needed to be coaxed out of their reluctance to stroke old Daniel the donkey, but he was the gentlest, most patient creature on the planet and once they had overcome their nervousness, they loved to watch him nibble on the carrots Joan provided for the children to feed the animals.

'Hi, Gran.' Angie strolled into the shop and helped herself to an apple.

'Missed breakfast,' she explained, her stunning smile lighting up her face as she sank her teeth into the pale flesh.

'No school today?' Joan asked.

Angie wandered towards the home bakery, eyed the cakes greedily then munched determinedly on her apple.

Angie had inherited her sense of chic from her French mother. Most of the other students who hung around the coffee bar in town were bundled up in scarves and lumpy sweaters and jeans. Angie wore a pink pashmina draped elegantly around her neck, an eye-catching contrast to her dark tank top. Her long legs were clad in dark, opaque tights and a cerise mini-skirt completed the ensemble.

'Pity Mum always insists on no cakes until tea time,' Angie grumbled through a mouthful of apple.

'That's why you have beautiful skin and a lovely figure,' Joan smiled at her. 'And you haven't answered my question.'

'I skipped class,' Angie confessed.

'It's only a tutorial.'

Joan bit down a sigh. 'Your mother won't like that,' she felt honour-bound to remind her granddaughter.

'Spare me the lecture, Gran.' Her blue eyes flashed a warning that told Joan she was close to overstepping the mark. At times Angie looked so like her father, Joan had to catch her breath. She'd often seen the same expression on Peter's face, usually when he and Richard were having a bit of a set-to. She couldn't count the number of times she'd had to intervene between father and son in an effort to keep the peace, and now her life had turned full circle and she was regularly playing the same role between mother and daughter.

It was no good Joan trying to explain to Elise that Angie was a growing girl and at times she needed to challenge authority.

'It's her role in life. It's healthy,' Joan would say. 'I'm sure you were the same when you were growing up. I know I

11

was.' Joan often recalled her own student days when a weekend wasn't complete without a protest march, a sit in or a rally.

'I never gave my parents any grief,' Elise had insisted.

'Not even when you wanted to marry my son?' she'd queried with a smile. 'An impoverished English artist?'

With a reluctant twinkle in her eyes, Elise had admitted, 'Well, maybe just that once. My father wasn't too happy, but things turned out all right in the end.'

'As they will with Angie,' she'd assured her.

Looking at her granddaughter today, Joan wished she felt more confident about Angie's future. It was all very well having causes, but at this time of her life she also needed to study if she wanted to pass her exams.

Ever since Elise had been widowed, she and Angie had occupied the flat above the farm shop, but more often than not, Angie would spend her nights in the spare bedroom of her grand-mother's adjacent cottage after another explosive exchange of views with her mother.

'Well, if you're not going to study today, you might as well make yourself useful. I'm not having you sitting around doing nothing all day and eating my profits.'

'Gra-a-n,' Angie protested.

'Call it work experience,' Joan said firmly. 'Maureen's at the dentist, so I need another pair of hands. Those potatoes need pricing and I'm short on tomatoes. You'll find the new delivery round the back.'

'Slave driver,' Angie grumbled. 'Where are you going?' she demanded as Joan headed out of the door.

'To check up on the school trip doing the nature trail. I like to make sure none of the stragglers have got lost.'

'I wondered what all the noise was about,' Angie grumbled. 'All that giggling woke me up.'

Joan raised her eyebrows as she

glanced at the wall clock. It was well past ten o'clock.

'I was late in last night that's why I overslept,' Angie admitted with a shamefaced look at her grandmother.

'Where's your mother?' Joan asked. 'I haven't seen her.'

'Neither have I, Gran. She must've gone out really early. I found a note on the kitchen table. She's helping the summer school administrator with some student application forms.'

'Right, well you know where to find me,' Joan said as she donned her high visibility gilet, embossed with the Trent farm shop logo. The reflective green of the tunic was easy to identify for any confused children or those who looked like they might stray from the official path.

Outside the scene that met her eyes was the usual one of chaotic confusion and Joan smiled as she watched excited children stroking the rabbits and laughing at Gertie's antics.

'Morning, Joan,' Harry called across

from where he was rolling the neighbouring cricket club pitch. 'Maureen won't be in today. She's sleeping off the effects of her injection.'

Joan waved to the club handyman and after telling him to give her best wishes for a speedy recovery to his wife Maureen, made her way over to the school party.

★   ★   ★

Elise chewed her pen as she looked out of the window. The April morning was bright with the promise of spring, but every so often a sudden shower soaked the college car park. Students hurried across the campus huddled under umbrellas as more dark clouds scudded across the sky.

It was on days like this she missed Peter so much. The wet weather never bothered him. He used to drag a protesting Elise out of the warmth of their flat and together they would walk for miles across the windswept Downs, enjoying the feel of the fresh air on their faces before they descended on a local inn for a hearty supper.

After years of living in England the weather didn't bother Elise any more. She no longer yearned for the Mediterranean heat of her home village, high up in the Alpes-Maritimes. These days she preferred the cool freshness of an English spring day.

Her mind wandered back to last night's marriage proposal from Mark. She hadn't slept well and her head ached from lack of sleep. Had she done the right thing turning him down?

Her daughter had introduced them at a parents' evening and even in the face of her subsequent denials, Elise still suspected Angelique of match-making. Kyle, Mark's son was in the same year and the two of them often went out together in a crowd.

Why then was she hesitating? There was no emotional baggage. Mark's ex-wife Amanda was a pleasant woman and in a new relationship and there was no question of Elise having been involved in the break up. Mark had told Elise that Amanda had been lonely when he worked nights out on patrol and after one broken family party too many, they had decided to go their separate ways, but it had been an amicable split.

Elise turned back to her desk. Daydreaming would not get the work done. Red tape could at times be extremely tedious, but it had to be completed. The reputation of the language college owed a lot of its pupil exchange success to her but some days she found checking up on the form filling more of a challenge than others.

Suddenly, her mobile phone sprang into life. 'Elise Trent,' she answered.

'Hi, Mum, it's me.'

'Angelique, where are you?' Elise was one of the few people who called Angie by her full name.

'Helping Gran out in the shop. It's a bit of a madhouse here today. Maureen's thrown a sicky because her teeth hurt and we've got hordes of children clambering all over the place. I'm thinking of throwing a sicky myself. You've no idea how heavy a boxes of tomatoes can be.'

'You have no classes today?'

Angie made a non-committal sound at the back of her throat.

'Could I have an advance on my allowance?' she asked before Elise could pursue the matter further. 'There's a gig in the park and the tickets cost an arm and a leg.'

'I do not wish you to go,' Elise replied firmly.

'Why not? Everyone else is.'

'You are not everyone else, Angelique. You need to study if you want to go to Fashion College. Don't think I haven't noticed you've been skipping tutorials.'

'I got straight A's in my mocks.'

'Only because you crammed.'

'So I'll cram again. Please, Mum,' Angie wheedled but her mother was one of the few people who could withstand her daughter's charm.

Elise could hear her daughter's heavy breathing down the line. She knew she was being strict but as a single parent of a wilful teenage daughter, she'd had to take the place of both mother and father, and at times it wasn't easy.

'Would you like some of my special bouillabaisse for supper?' she asked in a softer voice. The mixed fish and shellfish stew was one of Angie's favourites.

'Not tonight, Mum. I'm going out,' she said.

'Where are you going?' Elise demanded.

'Don't worry. I won't go near the park. I'll hang out with the gang in the coffee bar.'

'I thought you said everyone was going to this gig.'

'So I tried it on,' Angie admitted. 'Bye. Love you.'

Elise switched off her mobile. When it came to winding her up, Angie knew how to press all the right buttons. A reluctant smile curved Elise's generous mouth. Truth be told, she quite enjoyed the stimulation of her daughter's challenges, even if at times they were exhausting. At least it kept her on her toes.

She clicked her mouse and re-addressed her attention to the latest pupil exchange application.

* * *

'What are you going to do?' Seth Baxter asked Joan over a cup of tea in her kitchen after she'd closed up for the day. A letter lay on the table between them.

'I wish I knew,' she admitted with a worried frown. 'Local feeling is running high and there are endless action groups set up against the scheme.'

Until now the land adjacent to Merritt's Wood had by mutual agreement always been used for rural activities, such as Joan's nature trails, to maintain the peace and tranquillity of the area.

Over the past few months Joan, along with the neighbouring cricket club, had received business communications asking if they were interested in selling off some of their land. This latest one was from a company who stated they had plans for a holiday caravan park. There was no denying the area would welcome an economic boost, and a caravan park would provide much needed employment.

'The cricket club committee are in a quandary,' Seth told her. 'We're split down the middle. The older members want nothing to do with the scheme and the younger ones think it's a good idea.'

'Which group do you fall into?'

'The worse one of the lot,' Seth's forehead creased as he admitted, 'I'm one of the don't knows.'

'At least they haven't put a time limit on their offer.'

'But they're not going to wait forever

are they? We've convened an extraordinary general meeting tomorrow night.'

'Will I be allowed to know the outcome?'

'Of course, after all you do have a vested interest.'

They drank their tea in companionable silence. Seth and Joan had first met when, as a fielder, he'd come searching for the team's cricket ball after an over enthusiastic batsman hit it over the boundary into her goat garden. It was with the greatest difficulty that they'd managed to persuade Gertie not to eat it and even trickier to get out of the compound with their dignity still intact — on a good day Gertie could butt for the county.

After much laughter and breathless manoeuvres Joan had accepted Seth's offer of a drink in the club after the match by way of apology for all the inconvenience caused. The drink had turned into a regular date and now they often went out for a meal together. Joan's name was on the tea roster and she attended most of the cricket club functions as Seth's partner.

'Well, I best get up to the allotment before the light goes from the day,' Seth said.

'Keep me posted,' Joan called after him.

'Will do,' he called back.

Not long after his departure, Elise poked her head round the kitchen door. 'Can you keep an eye on Angelique for me tonight, Joan? There's been an accident down by the ferry. I think a French car was driving on the wrong side of the road. It doesn't sound serious but I never know how long I'm going to be. It all depends on how many people are involved. Angelique knows where I am; I've just spoken to her. She's going to a student meeting and will come over afterwards if that's all right?'

'I'll keep an eye out for her,' Joan promised. 'Are you going out with Mark later?'

'I don't think so.'

'Everything is all right between the pair of you?' Joan asked, noting Elise's quick frown.

'Absolutely,' she smiled. 'I must go. I'm late already.'

As she drove out of the car park, Joan could not shake off the suspicion that her daughter-in-law was not telling the truth.

2

It was the usual bustling scenario down by the ferry terminal. The blue and white tape surrounding the crime scene flapped in the breeze. Elise's suspicions had indeed been correct. A French driver, confused by a roundabout and with a not terribly good knowledge of the English language had somehow got himself on the wrong side of the road, then swerved into the oncoming lane in an attempt to right himself.

Luckily it had been a quiet time of day and no one had been injured but the front wing of his car had been dented when he came into contact with a lamp post and the police had been called in. The driver was now sitting on the side of the road, with his head in his hands, while everyone waited for Elise to arrive.

It would be her job as official

interpreter to make sure the Frenchman knew exactly what was going on and to inform him of arrangements for his car to be towed to a local garage.

She was greeted by a police officer, a colleague of Mark's. 'Hello, Elise. Nothing too complicated here I don't think.' He looked at his notes. 'As I understand it, the driver was confused about driving on the left, usual story. Purely routine, I'd say. We've phoned a garage and they'll take the car away shortly.'

'The driver is not being charged?'

'No, not at the moment, but we want to be sure he understands the situation, and of course we need to check his documents and paperwork.' He checked his notes again. 'He's a Jacques Dubois from your neck of the woods, I understand.'

'My what?' Elise frowned, not understanding the expression.

'A small village in the Alpes-Maritimes, it says here. My knowledge of French is limited, but it seems he drove up through France yesterday then the Channel was a bit choppy so he didn't get much rest on the ferry. It's no wonder he was disorientated.'

The man in question looked up with a guilty expression on his face as Elise approached him. 'Bonjour, Monsieur Dubois. It is all right,' she reassured him in his native tongue, 'you are not in any trouble.'

'You are French?' he asked in relief.

'I am and I'm here to make sure you understand exactly what is happening.'

'I speak some English, but everyone talks too fast, and some of their expressions I do not understand.'

Elise sympathised with him. Even now there were occasions when even after many years of living in England, she didn't always understand what was being said.

'I am told you come from the Alpes-Maritimes,' she said in an attempt to relax him.

The guilty expression instantly

returned to the driver's face. 'Why do you ask?'

'I too come from that part of France.'

'I'm sorry. I can't think straight.' Jacques Dubois passed a hand over his brow. He seemed to be avoiding looking Elise in the eye. 'You are police?'

'No. I'm a freelance translator.'

'It all happened so quickly,' Monsieur Dubois mumbled. He seemed to be talking to himself and Elise noticed he was perspiring and trying to undo his tie.

'Would you like me to book you into a room for the night?' she suggested. 'You should get some rest. I know a convenient bed and breakfast nearby. I could check to see if they have a room vacant? Then perhaps in the morning you can continue on your journey when your car is repaired? Where were you going before the accident?' Elise asked.

'Er . . . to visit friends,' was the uncertain reply.

'You are here on holiday?'

'Yes . . . No . . . Why are you asking all these questions?'

Sensing Monsieur Dubois might still be in a state of shock Elise decided to keep the interview as short as possible. 'If I could just check your paperwork?' she asked.

'Is that really necessary?'

'Now, your name is Jacques Dubois?' Elise queried ignoring the question.

'I need to make a telephone call.' Jacques Dubois tried to snatch up his mobile which was balanced on his briefcase and which Elise was using as a makeshift surface for her form filling.

'All in good time,' Elise insisted.

'But it's important.' He made another grab for the phone. In the ensuing tussle the briefcase slipped off Elise's lap and onto the ground. As it fell open the wind whipped some of the contents into the air.

'This is all your fault!' Jacques Dubois shouted at Elise.

The police traffic officer was by their

side in an instant. 'It's all right, sir.' He did his best to quieten the agitated Frenchman. 'Nothing to get worked up about. You okay, Elise?'

'I'm fine,' she replied, dusting herself down before scooping up the Frenchman's belongings and the contents of her handbag, which were also scattered along the grass verge.

'If you're finished up here, Elise, we should get Monsieur Dubois to Casualty for a check up.'

'Good idea,' Elise agreed with him. She lowered her voice as she said, 'He seems to be acting a bit odd; perhaps he banged his head on the windscreen or something?'

'Shock can affect people in different ways.'

'I've filled in his paperwork as best I can.' Elise passed the forms over to the policeman.

'Thanks, Elise. Take care. Sorry we kept you so long.'

★ ★ ★

'What time did Angelique get home last night?' Elise enquired the next morning when she joined Joan for a cup of coffee in the shop.

'I'm not sure exactly,' Joan evaded a direct answer.

The truth was Angie had been rather late and Joan had been on the point of telephoning the Principal when the sound of car tyres outside had announced her return.

'Kyle's father gave me a lift,' she'd announced as she breezed in.

'Isn't Mark coming in?' Joan had asked in surprise. 'Elise should be back soon.'

'Said he needed to get home. I am starving. What's to eat?'

Now, to Joan's relief, Elise seemed disinclined to pursue the matter of Angie's late night. Joan was wondering how to voice her concern about the situation between Elise and Mark when Elise asked, 'It's the cricket club meeting tonight, is it not?'

'It's meetings all the time at the

moment,' Joan sighed. 'I don't know if I'm coming or going. I can't keep up with them all.'

'Have you heard anything about a student protest?' Elise asked, 'To do with the proposed development?'

Angie had sworn her grandmother to secrecy when she had revealed her involvement with the college action group. Joan felt that keeping the peace between her daughter-in-law and granddaughter was at times akin to tightrope walking.

'I suppose students need a cause, don't they?' she said by way of reply, anxious not to betray Angie's trust.

Whilst sympathising with her grand-daughter's views, Joan had stressed she would only honour Angie's confidence as long as the protest was a peaceful one. It was at times like this that Joan missed Richard more than ever. With his keen business brain he would have immediately been able to decide on the best course of action to take without resorting to action groups and mass protests. Their Beech Mead neighbours would have listened to Richard. His was always the voice of reason.

'We still haven't had my fish stew supper,' Elise mused, changing the subject as she finished her coffee.

'How about tonight if you're not doing anything?' Joan suggested. 'You're not going out with Mark?' It was none of her business, she knew, but there were dark circles under Elise's eyes and she didn't like to think of her being unhappy.

'I could get some shellfish at the market today in my lunch hour,' Elise replied, ignoring Joan's question.

Realising her questions weren't welcome, Joan replied, 'I'll provide the vegetables from the shop. I've got some early new potatoes and the baby lettuces are fresh in.'

The sound of an arriving coach drew their attention to the car park. Joan checked her watch. 'That'll be my morning tour.'

'Then I'd better leave you to it.' Elise

picked up her handbag. 'Is Maureen fully recovered from her toothache? I haven't seen her around.'

'I sent her home. She's still looking a bit peaky. Gary said he would stay on until lunch time.'

Elise made a face at the mention of Maureen's son.

'What have you got against the poor boy?' Joan demanded. 'He's young and strong, even if he does need a bit of guidance now and then.'

'I cannot help suspecting he only hangs around here in the hope of catching a glimpse of my Angelique.'

'So do half the young lads in her class,' Joan chided her daughter-in-law. 'It's natural. She is bright and friendly.'

'And beautiful,' Elise added.

'There's nothing wrong with that.'

'I know,' Elise admitted with a shamefaced smile, 'but I don't want my little girl growing up too fast.'

'She's seventeen and not so little any more. She needs to spread her wings.

You can't tie her to your apron strings forever.'

'That doesn't stop me worrying. There are so many temptations for young people these days, more than there were when I was her age.' Elise looked no more than a young girl herself as she confessed her fears to Joan.

She patted Elise's hand. 'Angie is a sensible, caring girl. Sometimes you have to trust to your child's common sense otherwise they will never learn what life is all about. She'll probably make a few mistakes along the way, but as long as she knows we'll always be here to pick up the pieces I don't think she'll come to any great harm.'

Elise lowered her voice. 'Gary Jenkins seems more than a little smitten with Angelique.'

'Well she's not here this morning, which is just as well as I think I'm going to have my hands full.'

Maureen's gangly son chose that moment to emerge from the back room carrying a box of lettuces. He glared balefully at Elise from behind his horn-rimmed glasses.

'There you are,' Joan greeted him brightly. 'I see you found the lettuces. After you've finished stocking up I'd like you to help man the till for a while this morning. Is that alright?'

''S alright,' he mumbled, head down, shuffling to the shop.

'I hope he didn't overhear us.' Elise followed his progress with a worried frown. 'I think I might have been a bit harsh on him and I wouldn't want to hurt his feelings,' Elise said.

'The young are resilient. I'll keep him busy. That should take his mind off Angie.'

A shadow appeared in the doorway blotting Joan's vision.

'Mrs Trent?'

With a sinking heart, Joan recognised the bulky form of Councillor Newman's wife.

'Good morning,' she replied.

'There was no one to greet us in the

car park when we arrived. That's really not good enough. The coach driver had no idea where to park.'

'I'm sorry. You did say eleven o'clock and it's only — '

'I would be grateful for your assistance, when you've finished your coffee,' she added with a pointed look at Joan's mug.

Joan bit down a retort. She had been up since six o'clock taking early deliveries and preparing for the day but she knew it wouldn't do to go upsetting the wife of one of Beech Mead's most eminent citizens.

'Bye, Joan, have a good morning.' Elise threw an impudent look at Mrs Newman's rather unattractive felt hat and gave a parting shot of, 'You know, blue really isn't your colour. Perhaps a soft peach might help tone down your healthy complexion?'

With a wink at Joan, Elise waved goodbye. Joan's lips twitched. At times Elise could be as mischievous as Angie.

'If you would like to assemble the

children at the meeting point, I'll be with you in a minute.' Joan decided it would be best to get on with the day.

For all her brisk efficiency Mrs Newman didn't seem to be totally in control of her party. With a great show of clapping her hands and bossing everyone around, she finally managed to quieten everyone down. 'Now, children,' she said in her carrying voice, 'this is Mrs Trent.'

'Good morning, Mrs Trent,' the children chanted in unison.

'Don't do that,' Joan said to a little boy who had wandered away from the group and was busy poking a stick through Gertie's fence and upsetting her.

'I'll discipline my own son, thank you.' Mrs Newman glared.

'Then would you please tell him for his own safety to stop tormenting the goats?'

'I hope your animals aren't dangerous.'

'Of course not, but they need to be

treated with respect.'

'My son is only playing; he's not harming the creature.' Mrs Newman made it sound as though the animal was unclean.

'Perhaps not, but the goat won't understand it's only a game,' Joan replied. 'Now will you stop him, or shall I?'

Mrs Newman strode over to her son.

'Can't you take charge?' Joan murmured to one of the teaching assistants.

'Mrs Newman stepped in at the last minute when one of the other parents had to pull out. The head teacher told us we weren't to upset her. The school has already had several altercations with her regarding young Alfie.'

'I can imagine,' Joan sympathised, 'but I won't have her Alfie upsetting my animals.'

'I'll try to keep an eye on him for you and make sure he doesn't cause any further trouble.'

'Right well if you need my help, I'll be in the shop. We're short handed too,'

Joan explained. She had intended escorting the tour, but ten minutes of Mrs Newman's company was already more than she could take.

*   *   *

It turned out to be an unusually busy morning. A high proportion of customers seemed to demand Joan's attention and with the constant ringing of the telephone she and Gary had their hands full. It was only during a brief lull in business that Joan was able to glance at the wall clock and realise that the tour had taken well over its allotted time.

'We're one missing,' the teaching assistant confided as Joan went to find out what was happening.

Before she could reply there was an outraged cry of indignation behind them. Joan whirled round to see Gertie head-butting her fence and trying to eat Alfie's pullover as he drove another stick through a gap in the palings.

'Let go, you brute!' Mrs Newman

charged over to wrestle with her son's jumper as Gertie's teeth found their target.

Obeying the authority in Mrs Newman's voice, Gertie immediately did as she was told and Mrs Newman and Alfie toppled backwards. Gales of laughter erupted from the children as Mrs Newman's felt hat fell off her head and landed on one of Gertie's horns. In the face of strong opposition from Alfie, Mrs Newman was doing her best to retain her dignity as her son, bellowing in outrage, struggled to retrieve his dropped stick.

Joan raced over and grabbed it from him. 'I'll have that if you don't mind.'

'This is outrageous,' Mrs Newman puffed up at her.

'So is your son's behaviour. I'd like you both to leave, now,' Joan insisted, anxious to defuse the situation before it spiralled out of control.

'Don't worry.' The councillor's wife managed to retrieve her hat from Gertie and rammed it back on her head.

'We're not staying — *and* I shall report you to the authorities for neglect.'

'I warned your son not to torment the animals,' Joan replied hotly. 'I can't be responsible if he chose to ignore me.'

'Don't think you've heard the last of this,' Mrs Newman threatened as she stormed towards her car, dragging her still wailing son after her.

* ★ ★ ★

'Poor you,' Angie sympathised over their bouillabaisse as Joan recounted the drama of the day. 'I remember Mrs Newman. She was always interfering when I was at junior school and that was years ago.'

'It is not right that she should threaten you,' Elise agreed. 'You do so much for the community. What does she do, apart from make a big noise and wear unattractive hats?'

'Big noises can often cause a lot of trouble,' Joan replied with a worried frown, 'but if she pushes me too far, I shall accept the developers latest offer for this caravan park thing, then she really will have something to shout about.'

'Joan, you wouldn't!'

'Gran!'

Her daughter-in-law and grand-daughter cast twin looks of outrage in her direction.

'Probably not . . . ' Joan calmed down a bit, 'But I do hope that husband of hers doesn't take things further.'

'He won't,' Angie replied, with all the confidence of youth. 'Tomorrow she'll most likely be upsetting someone else anyway. Now come on, Mum,' she turned to Elise, 'where's this peach Pavlova you promised us for dessert? You didn't forget the cream, did you?'

★ ★ ★

Elise frowned at the pocketbook as it slid out of her handbag and onto the bedroom carpet. She bent down to pick it up and turned it over in her hands. It was good quality woven leather and continental in design. She unclipped the fastener and looked inside. The credit card indicated it belonged to Jacques Dubois and she realised she must have scooped it up with her own things following the tussle with his briefcase.

She should return it to the police but after her two glasses of wine with dinner she was reluctant to drive down to the station. Her fingers hovered over Mark's speed dial number. There was no message from him in her voicemail and she hadn't heard from him since she'd turned down his marriage proposal. Deciding it was only fair to let him make the first move she reluctantly switched off her phone.

She hadn't expected to miss his company quite so much.

Searching in another pocket of the wallet Elise found a business card displaying a French telephone number. Perhaps for the moment the best thing to do would be to ring the number and leave a message; if someone were picking up calls then they would be able to contact Jacques with the good news that his wallet had been found. Elise dialled the number. A man answered on the second ring.

'Good evening,' she began, 'My name is Elise Trent. You don't know me but I have Mr Dubois' pocket book.'

'You have found it?' The voice sounded relieved.

'Yes. I do apologise but I seem to have picked it up in error.'

'I was so worried when I lost it.'

'You lost it?' Elise asked confused.

'Yes.' The voice down the end of the line sounded equally puzzled. 'That is what you are ringing about?'

'You are back home already?'

'I've been out all day . . . but . . . yes, I am back home.'

Elise's confusion deepened. 'I'm sorry. I don't understand. Back home from where?'

'Work of course.'

'When exactly did you lose your wallet?' Elise asked.

'A month ago in Nice. It's very busy there this time of year with all the tourists and regrettably I think I was the victim of a pickpocket. Is that where you are — in Nice?'

'No, monsieur. I'm in England.'

'England?' It was the man's turn to sound confused.

'You are Jacques Dubois?' Elise asked.

'Yes, I am, of course.'

'And you weren't involved in a traffic accident yesterday after you drove off the cross channel ferry?'

'No madame, I was not. I do not drive a car and I have never been to England in my life.'

3

Elise had never visited Mark at work before and now, seated opposite him in the interview room, she felt unaccountably nervous. A woman police officer sat impassively in a corner surveying the proceedings but saying nothing.

'I would have reported it before,' Elise said, 'only I was rather busy. Joan's been single-handed in the shop because Maureen hasn't been well and I've been helping out when I have a spare moment.' Elise decided not to mention the trouble she had also been having with her daughter. Since the night of Mark's proposal everything seemed to have gone wrong. 'I put it away and quite simply I forgot about it. It was only today when I was sorting out my bag that I realised I still had it.'

Mark looked carefully through the

contents of the wallet before replacing them.

'You say the real Monsieur Dubois told you he had never been to England?'

Elise watched the light flicker on the recording device. 'Yes. I telephoned the number on that business card.'

'And Monsieur Dubois thinks he was the victim of a pickpocket in Nice?'

'That's what he told me. Have you spoken to the other Monsieur Dubois — the one I interviewed down by the ferry?' Elise asked.

'Unfortunately he discharged himself from Casualty before we or the insurance company had a chance to speak to him.'

'He's disappeared?' Elise blinked. 'What about the contact address he gave?'

'It was false. We checked it out. So it seems your Monsieur Dubois was telling the truth.'

'There's nothing more I can add to my statement,' Elise said after reading through a typewritten copy of her comments.

'Then perhaps you would sign and date it,' Mark replied, offering her a pen.

'Is that all?' She asked as she signed.

'For now. We may need to call you if we trace the miscreant.' Mark said as he put all the papers in a folder and switched off the recorder. 'Now, how about a cup of tea in the canteen?'

Elise was pleased to escape the confines of the interview room. Although she had attended many such interviews before as an interpreter, the experience as a witness left her unsettled.

Neither spoke as they travelled down in the lift. Elise had not expected their first meeting after she had turned down Mark's proposal to be like this.

The steamy warmth of the canteen provided a welcome change to the stark functionality of the interview room. Down here everything seemed reassuringly normal. Groups of people gossiped at tables and a radio played in the background.

'I got you a cream cake as well,' Mark replied. 'I don't know about you but I could do with an injection of something sweet and we both missed lunch.'

'Thank you,' Elise smiled up at him. It was good to see him. 'How's Kyle?' she asked as she nibbled at her éclair. 'Is he studying hard for his exams?'

Mark made a face. 'Have you heard about this demonstration he's got himself involved in?'

Elise dabbed at her lips with her paper serviette. 'Sorry, I seem to be in a bit of a mess. I always get cream everywhere.'

'That's part of the fun of eating an eclair. Here, you've missed a bit.' Mark leaned forward and with the serviette wiped cream off her chin. 'Want me to get you another one? A serviette, not a cake I mean. There's enough cream in that one to fill two cakes as it is.'

'I'll manage,' Elise replied with a light laugh. She wished Mark would stop looking at her so intently and that the touch of his fingertips wasn't having such a disturbing effect on her.

'Angelique's head teacher called me,' she added.

Mark raised his eyebrows. 'What has she been up to?'

'It seems instead of getting down to her studies, she's been more interested in arranging a protest rally.'

'Regarding the proposed development of Merritt's Wood? The plans indicate the developers would be sympathetic to the natural habitat.'

'They would say that wouldn't they?' Elise replied. 'But it's stirred up a lot of local feeling.'

'I suppose they would,' Mark agreed. 'So the youngsters have set up a protest group?'

'It seems my daughter is one of the ringleaders.'

'Kyle's been doing his bit as well. They're printing leaflets and flyers. He says it's all part of his citizenship awareness. I suppose I can't argue with that one.'

'Joan's not helping either. She sympathises with them.'

'I thought the developers had approached her personally. Doesn't her land back onto the wood?'

'Yes, it does, but she was a bit of a rebel in her youth. She's taking the students' side. I fully expect to see her parading through the town carrying a placard, or some such. Did anyone ever have such a family as mine?'

Mark smiled in sympathy. 'There I was thinking your mother-in-law was a pillar of the community.'

'She is, but in their student days she and my father-in-law used to travel round the country on protest marches. They only really settled down when Peter was born.'

'Good for her,' Mark acknowledged with a smile. 'As a serving police officer I know I shouldn't say this, but we need people like her to stand up for their rights.'

'Don't you start,' Elise complained. 'I'm having enough trouble trying to keep my daughter in order. Seriously Mark, I don't like her getting involved in something, well, unpleasant.'

'Kyle assures me it's all going to be very low key so I don't think you need be worried.'

'I can't help it,' Elise replied. 'When Angelique gets a bee in her bonnet, there's no stopping her. At this time of her life she should be studying for her future. She wants to go to fashion college but she won't pass the entrance exam if she doesn't get good grades on her course work. I've tried putting my foot down, but all we seem to do these days is have words.'

'It's part of growing up. It's a daughter's duty to disagree with her mother, isn't it?'

'She used to be such a good girl,' Elise said. 'I don't know what's got into her lately.'

'Would you like me to talk to Kyle? He may have some-influence with Angie.'

'Would you?' Elise looked hopefully

at Mark. 'I don't want things getting out of hand.'

'Amanda's going away so Kyle is staying with me this weekend. Leave it with me.'

Elise wanted to convince herself that her heightened colour was from the steamy canteen, but she knew it wasn't; it had taken an enforced separation from Mark to make her realise how much he meant to her.

'Why haven't you been in touch?' Elise asked, reapplying her attention to her cake.

'Have you missed me?' Mark asked, leaning forward.

'Yes.' Elise had never been one for subterfuge.

After a short pause, Mark said, 'I'm moving out of the flat.'

'You're leaving?' Elise gulped down the last of her cake.

'Kyle will be spending more time with me and my flat really isn't big enough for two. I've been looking at a few properties.'

'I see. Have you seen anything you like?'

'Not yet. I've been a bit tied up with a spate of antique clock thefts in the area.'

'Joan was telling me one of her customers lost a Vienna Regulator that was old and quite valuable.'

'We think they're being stolen to order and taken abroad. Being so close to the channel ports, it's easy for the perpetrators to be out of the country before the theft is even discovered if the owners are away.'

'You think they're operating on the south coast?'

'Possibly. That's why I was intrigued when the fake Monsieur Dubois disappeared.'

'Do you think he is part of the ring?'

'I don't know, but something's not right.' Mark paused. 'I was wondering . . . There's no connection between you, is there?'

Elise frowned. 'I don't understand.'

'You and he come from the same area of France.'

'We don't know that. The man in the accident was in possession of another man's wallet. Besides I've not lived in France for a long time. Why should I know him?'

'Oh, no reason . . . ' Mark admitted rather unconvincingly.

Elise took a deep breath to control her raging thoughts. 'Mark, I resent the implication that I might be involved with a shady antiques dealer.'

'That's not what I meant at all,' Mark protested, his raised voice causing several heads to turn in their direction. 'I only wondered if you recognised him, that's all.'

'Well, I don't.' Elise glanced at the wall clock. 'I have to go. Thank you for the tea and cake.'

She stood up, anxious now to distant herself from Mark. His suspicions had provided a good excuse for her to accept that their personal relationship was over. Obviously she had wounded his pride turning down his proposal.

'Elise, I . . . ' Mark began but his

pager bleeped. 'I have to go,' he said. 'I'll be in touch.'

★　★　★

Elise welcomed the feel of fresh air on her face. It gave her a chance to calm down as she made her way to her car. It was a natural assumption of Mark's to imagine she might have known Jacques Dubois; all the same, sometimes his police mind suspected innocent people of being involved in underhand activities. Until now she had always assumed she didn't fit into that category.

Elise yanked open her driver's door. Why was life so complicated? Was Mark really behaving like this because she had dented his male pride? She would have expected him to be more adult in his behaviour.

Elise started her car and drove off in the direction of the town. A group of students were congregating around the bandstand and handing out leaflets. There was no sign of Angie for which

Elise was grateful.

Mrs Nelson, the head teacher had explained to Elise that Angie had always been one of her brightest pupils. With her flair for colour and natural sense of style she had been hoping Angie would qualify for a place at fashion college, but lately her course work had been suffering due to her extra curricular activities.

While Mrs Nelson hadn't said so in as many words, Elise suspected her daughter was in danger of being kept back a year, unless her work improved.

It was at times like this Elise missed Mark's influence. Angie listened to him and without any other significant male in her life he had provided a balanced view on some of her student problems. He could say things to her that her own mother couldn't. It helped with Kyle being in the same year. The two males were occasionally like a father and brother to her. Until recently the four of them had often gone out together, if Kyle was staying over with his father.

Elise bit her lip. Perhaps her daughter had expected Elise to accept Mark's proposal of marriage. It was possible she had found out about it from Kyle, although she doubted that Mark would have told his son he intended to propose before he had spoken to Elise. Whatever, she supposed Mark would now prefer to go out with Kyle on his own. The house move too would take up more of his time.

Elise drove into the farm shop car park. It was deserted and she was surprised to find it was already closed up for the day. Mondays were often their quietest day and she supposed Joan had closed promptly at five. Seeing a light on in the kitchen she headed towards it. Although Joan lived in an adjacent cottage she often did her paperwork in the shop.

'Hello, I'm back,' she called out. 'Any tea on the go?'

Joan looked up in surprise. 'I didn't expect you so soon.'

Seth was sitting opposite Joan at the

kitchen table. Elise couldn't help noticing they were holding hands. 'Did I interrupt something?' she asked.

The pair of them looked faintly embarrassed, like teenagers caught kissing on the sofa by one of their parents.

Seth greeted her with his friendly smile. 'I'd like you to the be the first to hear our news.'

Elise looked from Seth to Joan then back to Seth again.

'News?' she echoed faintly.

'I've asked Joan to marry me — and she has agreed!'

4

Joan's raised voice as she called up the stairs sounded urgent. Stifling a sigh, Elise called down, 'I'm in the lounge.'

She didn't add that she was catching up on urgent paperwork, but Joan's interruption couldn't have come at a more inconvenient time. That was the trouble with working from home; everyone assumed she was available to help out in the shop at a moment's notice. It was for this reason Elise often chose to work in the college library, or if that wasn't possible, go to a coffee bar with Internet access.

'Have you looked out of the window?' A breathless Joan charged into the flat.

Elise blinked at her. 'What happened to your blouse?' she asked. It was covered in earth and her trousers were stained.

'I dropped a sack of potatoes.' Joan flapped her hands. 'Never mind that — look.'

Elise followed the direction of Joan's pointed finger. 'The cricket club?'

'Exactly. The pitch. Someone's dug up a section overnight! Did you hear anything?'

Elise shook her head. She had been exhausted by recent events and, after several restless nights, had finally fallen asleep the moment her head touched the pillow. 'Sorry. No.'

'Seth's called the police. He's doing a check to see if anything else has been vandalised.'

'Who would do a thing like that?' Elise asked, all thoughts of work forgotten, 'And why?'

'I don't know but Seth's on the war path. The season is due to start shortly and it takes ages to get his pitch right.'

'Is it something to do with their meeting do you think? They ruled in favour of further talks with the developers, didn't they?'

'That information was supposed to be confidential. How did you find out?'

'Angelique told me.'

'How did she know?' Joan asked.

'Nothing's confidential for long when you've got a computer. I expect one of the students posted it on the net.'

'Surely this wasn't a student?' Joan looked shocked.

'I hope not,' Elise ran a hand through her hair, 'but it has to be someone local, unless it's a random act of vandalism.'

'This is all very unsettling.' Joan took another exhasperated look out of the window.

'Has anything been interfered with in the shop?' Elise asked.

Joan shook her head. 'Maureen did a quick check. The animals are fine and no windows were broken.'

'Do you want me to come down?' Elise asked.

'There's nothing you can do, I don't think,' Joan replied. 'If you're free later, join us for coffee. Mark said he would be over as soon as he could.'

'Thank you. I will.' Elise glanced back at her papers.

'I won't keep you,' Joan took the hint. 'I presume Angie has gone to college today?'

Elise nodded. 'And she wasn't out late last night, either. She spent the evening studying. I will ask her when she gets back to see if she knows anything about it, but I'm sure she doesn't.'

'I agree. Damaging property is not her thing.'

After Joan had gone Elise sat thoughtfully in her chair. With her concentration broken it was not easy to get back to her paperwork anyway. Things were turning nasty. She had no idea local feeling was running so high. Although she hadn't said so as she didn't want to alarm Joan, the shop was in a vulnerable position. News had got round about Joan's engagement to Seth and whoever last night's perpetrators were they might use the connection between the cricket club and the shop to inflict damage on farm property. Elise decided she would take a walk round later and check on the security of the sheds. One or two of the locks were a bit flimsy and wouldn't present much of a challenge to a determined intruder. Perhaps Harry or Seth could get some new ones.

Turning her attention back to her paperwork, she began to sort through the rest of her accounts, when another tap on the door disturbed her. She glanced at her watch and saw to her surprise it was nearly twelve o'clock.

'Sorry, Joan,' she called out. 'I forgot our coffee. Come in.'

There was a movement in the doorway. 'It's me.'

Mark entered the room and it seemed to shrink in his presence. The flat was not large at the best of times, really only big enough for herself and Angie.

Elise felt unaccountably nervous as she looked up at him. She hoped Mark wasn't going to accuse her of being involved in this latest incident. They hadn't spoken since their encounter in the canteen and Mark's words still rankled.

'I've, er, come to apologise.' He shifted his feet nervously.

Elise widened her eyes. 'You have?'

'Yes.' Mark now looked as uncomfortable as Elise felt.

'Sit down,' Elise said. 'I'm getting a crick in my neck. Here.'

She leaned forward and moved a pile of papers off a chair. Mark sank into it and it creaked under his weight as he cleared his throat again. 'I had no right to accuse you of being in cahoots with Jacques Dubois. I'm sorry. I realise now it was a stupid thing to say.'

'It was,' Elise smiled. 'But I accept your apology.'

She was glad Mark had the courage to admit he was wrong and she wasn't about to make him squirm any more. She had been annoyed at the time, but her temper, quick to erupt, always cooled down just as quickly and she realised she had possibly over reacted to his innocent remarks.

'I'm glad about that,' Mark said with obvious relief. 'There have been no further developments, by the way. I'll let you know if there are.'

'So ... the cricket pitch, what happened there?'

'Harry Jenkins says it was actually a very neat job. The bit of turf they cut out was placed in front of the club house and he thinks he can put it back where it came from, so no real damage has been done.' Mark shook his head. 'But I'm as puzzled as everyone else as to why they did it. It can't have been a prank because whoever did it brought their own spade.'

'They did?'

'Harry checked his shed and nothing's been used.'

'Stranger and stranger.'

'Joan said you didn't hear or see anything last night?'

'Sorry, no, but I'll keep a look out

tonight if you like.'

'I've arranged for a patrol car to keep an eye out. Don't go putting yourself in danger — if you see anything suspicious, you ring me immediately.'

'Of course,' Elise nodded.

'I've already told Joan not to go getting ideas either.'

'I hope you were firm with her,' Elise couldn't help a smile softening her lips. 'Otherwise she'll be out there with a spade setting about the intruders.'

'I'm relying on you,' Mark said with an answering smile, 'to keep the Trent women in order.'

It was good to be talking to Mark again. Elise enjoyed his company and she was glad they had cleared the air between them. 'How's the house hunting going?' she asked.

'It's a tedious business,' Mark admitted, 'and I've had other priorities. Kyle stayed over at the weekend. Amanda said he's going through a bit of a difficult phase with her so we had a man-to-man talk. He'd like to go into the police force but Amanda's not keen. I can understand how she feels but Kyle's got to do what he wants with his life, hasn't he?' He sighed. 'It's not easy being parents to teenage children, is it?' They smiled in complicity. 'How's Angie? I haven't seen her recently.'

'She's very involved with this action group, it seems.'

'Kyle mentioned that as well. He said he's keeping an eye on her for you. She hasn't been involved in anything more damaging than painting a few banners for demonstrations.'

'They couldn't have been involved in last night's incident?'

'I doubt it. Kyle definitely not, he was with Amanda.'

'And Angelique was with me — we had a fish stew supper and Joan joined us.'

'So, we've all got rock solid alibis,' Mark joked.

'Except you,' Elise countered. 'Where were you last night?'

'I ordered an Indian takeaway then I

watched some football and drank some beer.'

'Pah,' Elise made a Gallic gesture with her shoulders. 'Not good enough, I think.'

'You're teasing me, aren't you?' Mark said with a slow smile.

'Yes,' she admitted. 'I'm getting a little of my own back.'

'Point taken. You'll have to take my word for it, I'm afraid. You know me — I'm so clumsy in the dark, I'd probably have fallen over the spade or hit my foot.'

'That I can believe.' Elise's glance strayed to a bookshelf they had put up together and they both laughed at the memory of how it had fallen down the moment Elise had tried to actually put any books on it. 'You are not one of nature's handymen.'

'Shall we do a family foursome again some time? Kyle and me, you and Angie?' he asked. 'It would help everybody bond?'

'That would be lovely,' Elise agreed.

'I've seen notices in town about the annual fair coming soon.'

'Aren't we a little old for helter skelters?' Mark complained.

'Of course not — don't be so stuffy! I like the . . . how you say . . . merry go round. And the candyfloss — it's very bad for the teeth I know, but once a year I see no harm.'

'It's a date then. I like toffee apples but the last time I ate one I spent a fortune at the dentist having fillings fixed.' Mark glanced at his watch. 'I'd better get back to the station. We're short-handed today. Something's happening at Hay Hall and several of our people have been seconded to security.'

'The new owners have decided to host the vegetable competition this year, and they've asked Joan to be a judge.'

'I've heard they're keen to integrate. I'm glad they've decided to take it on after the previous people moved out. It's been empty far too long. I'll have to go up there and introduce myself some time. Best be off.'

Elise stood up and Mark brushed her cheeks in a casual kiss before ducking his head and making his way downstairs and out into the car park. Elise watched him from her window and waved as he looked up.

'Sorry to disturb you.' Another voice made her jump.

'It seems to be my morning for visitors,' she said with a smile. Maureen Jenkins now stood in the doorway, an anxious look on her face.

'Can I come in?'

'Of course. Are you feeling better now?' Elise prompted when Maureen frowned.

Her face cleared. 'Yes, I'm fine now, thank you.'

'Good.' She looked expectantly at Maureen. 'Did you wish to see me about something?'

Maureen sat down in the seat recently vacated by Mark and leaning forward, lowered her voice as if she were scared of being overheard. 'I'm worried about Joan.'

'Joan? Why?'

'Not just Joan — her and Seth, actually . . . This engagement.'

'You don't approve?'

'It's not that. I'm very pleased for them both. Only . . . ' she hesitated, 'Seth's got his own place in the town and, well . . . I wondered what they're going to do after they're married.'

'I haven't discussed it with Joan.'

'Do you think the shop will close?'

'I'm sure Joan won't want to close up. The shop is her life.'

'There was all that business with Mrs Newman and the goat. I gather it was quite unpleasant . . . '

'She is a big noise that one,' Elise dismissed Maureen's fears with an airy wave of her hand, 'but that is all. I'm sure it will come to nothing.'

Maureen did not look convinced. 'Even if it doesn't, we've got the development hanging over our heads. Harry said the cricket club didn't rule against it.'

'Is there anyone who doesn't know what happened at this supposedly private meeting?' Elise asked in exasperation.

'I was doing the refreshments, so I overheard bits. It was quite lively and people spoke up for both sides.'

'All we can do is wait and see,' Elise replied. 'Would you like me to have a word with Joan about her plans?'

'I don't want you to think I'm being nosey or anything like that,' Maureen said, 'only jobs are hard to come by. I like working here and what with Harry's maintenance work at the club, it's so convenient. Gary likes working Saturdays in the shop, too.' Elise flushed at the mention of Maureen's son, remembering her remarks about his lack of social skills. 'He and your Angie get along very well and I think it's good for him to have company his own age, especially as he doesn't have a girlfriend — ' Maureen gasped and quickly added, 'Not that I'm suggesting there's anything of that nature between your Angie and my Gary. It's just that some of the other students laugh at him a bit, but your Angie never does. She's a good, kind girl.'

Elise's heart went out to the raw-boned woman sitting opposite her. In many ways she was like her son; unsure of herself socially but pleasant and hard working. Elise did not like to think of her being worried about her future.

'I don't think you've any reason to be concerned,' she assured her. 'Seth likes living in Beech Mead and I'm sure it's not his intention to stop Joan working here, or to take over in any way. My mother-in-law is a very strong-minded person and she's put a lot into the business; it's not something she'd give up lightly. We're all settled here, the whole family, so in my opinion your job is perfectly safe.'

'Oh, you have taken a weight off my mind,' Maureen smiled happily. 'Talking to you always makes me feel better. I expect it's because you're French — you look at things differently, I mean, you not being local.'

Elise's smile was a little forced. Although Maureen had not meant any malice, Elise had been living in Beech Mead for many years, longer than some of the locals, but she was still regarded as an incomer by certain sections of the community. After Maureen made her way back to the shop Elise stifled a sigh. Her father had been right about their English neighbours. He had often advised his daughter that they were a race he would never totally understand and, at times, although she loved her adopted country as much as her native one, neither would she.

5

The sound of a telephone ringing dragged Elise from the depths of her sleep. She rolled over and blinked at the alarm clock. It showed five minutes past midnight.

'Hello?' she croaked into the receiver.

'The donkeys are out.' It was Joan's voice, sounding equally shaky. 'Someone's set them free.'

Elise was instantly alert and scrambled into her clothes.

'Angelique!' She raced into her daughter's bedroom. 'Quick, get up! Emergency! It's the donkeys.'

She switched on the light. Her daughter's bedclothes were disturbed but she wasn't there and her pyjamas were strewn across the floor.

Grabbing up a torch Elise raced out into the night. She could hear the donkeys braying in the distance and a shadowy figure seemed to be chasing after them.

'Hey, you! Stop at once!' Elise ran after him, her breath coming in short sharp bursts.

'Elise?' she heard Joan calling her name behind her but she didn't stop.

Gaining ground she caught up with the hooded figure. He had one of the donkeys by its halter. 'What do you think you're doing?' she demanded yanking him back by his collar. His hood fell off and Elise shone the torch into his face.

'Kyle?' she gasped in shocked surprise at Mark's son. 'What are you doing here?'

'I'm trying to rescue them. Someone let them out.'

Elise was in no mood to listen to his protestations of innocence. 'It was you!' Her voice was high with accusation.

'No, it wasn't,' he protested. 'Stop shaking me!'

'Where's Angie? What have you done with my daughter?'

'Nothing! Let me go!'

'There's a light on in the clubhouse,' Joan panted up to them as Kyle struggled to escape from Elise's grasp. 'Look — quick!' Joan ran off in the direction of the cricket club and Elise dropped her hold on Kyle and headed off in hot pursuit of her mother-in-law, leaving a gasping Kyle to marshal up the donkeys.

'Caught you!' Joan was first to tumble through the doors of the clubhouse. Daubed on a far wall in red paint was the slogan, *No To The Development*.

And standing beside it, clutching a tin of red paint and a brush, was Angie.

★   ★   ★

They were all sitting in the farm shop kitchen drinking tea, Joan, Elise, Kyle, Angie and Mark.

'We didn't do it,' Angie insisted.

'So what were you doing roaming about Farm Lane at midnight?' Mark demanded, looking at Kyle.

'I'd been working late at college.'

'Not until midnight. You know the rules during term time; you have to be back before ten unless there's a good reason. I put my trust in you,' Mark said, 'and you let me down.'

Kyle cast a glance at Angie.

'We'd been out together and Kyle saw me home,' Angie offered by way of explanation.

'You were supposed to be studying in your room,' Elise's voice rose in anger. 'I trusted you, too.'

'I did . . . I was . . . but Kyle sent me a text about half past nine. We met up to talk.'

'I won't have you going out without telling me what you're doing,' Elise was seriously angry now, 'and what was so important you had to talk about it until midnight?'

'We were back earlier,' Angie insisted. 'I knew you wouldn't understand,' her voice now rose to equal that of her mother's, 'You never do. You always think I'm up to no good.'

'Can this wait until another time?' Mark asked. 'We need to focus on priorities.'

'Mark's right, dear,' Joan patted Elise's arm before she flared up at Mark. 'Now's not the right moment. Angie's safe and that is all that matters.'

'Don't worry, I'll read Kyle the riot act too,' Mark smiled at Elise, 'but our first priority is to know exactly what has been going on. Kyle, you first.'

'I don't know,' Kyle admitted. 'Like Angie said, we walked home together. It was about ten, Dad, honest. Anyway I made sure Angie was indoors okay and then I began to walk back up the lane and something caught my attention.'

'Be more specific,' Mark interrupted.

'A noise, I think. I got the feeling someone might be up to no good, so I hid in the bushes. After a while nothing happened and I was about to give up when one of the donkeys rushed past me. It gave me a shock, I can tell you.'

'I'd just got into bed when I heard all

the commotion,' Angie put in, 'so I raced downstairs.'

'Why didn't you call me?' Elise demanded.

'There wasn't time, Mum. Besides I knew you'd go on about me having been out earlier . . . sorry, Mum,' she smiled across the table. 'I do love you and nothing happened, honest.'

Elise took a deep breath. A part of her wanted to crush her beautiful daughter to her chest, but another part wanted to shout at her for causing so much worry.

'What were you doing with that tin of paint?' she demanded.

'Like Gran I saw the light on in the clubhouse. I don't know who was there because the light went off as I pushed open the door. I turned it back on and then I saw that someone had been daubing paint on the wall. I don't know why I picked up the tin, I just did, and that's when Gran came charging in. I must say your language can be quite colourful at times, Gran.' She grinned at Joan who shifted uncomfortably in her chair. 'I had no idea you possessed such a vocabulary.'

'I was taken unawares,' Joan said in an attempt to justify her earlier tirade.

'It's a natural reaction to pick up evidence,' Mark said to Angie, 'I only hope you haven't obliterated any other fingerprints on the paint tin.' He turned to Kyle. 'Did you get all the donkeys back in?'

'Elise and I managed it between us after she came back from the clubhouse.'

'It was not easy, but I've checked and none are missing.'

'I'm annoyed that someone would interfere with the animals.' Joan was still very pink in the face. 'If I find out who's responsible, they'll get a piece of my mind.'

'Did the patrol car see anything?' Elise asked Mark.

He shook his head. 'They last did a tour about half past ten and reported nothing unusual. It must have been after that when Kyle thought he heard something.'

'I think it's time everyone went to bed.' Joan stood up. 'Otherwise we'll all be fit for nothing in the morning.'

Mark followed her example. 'I'll keep you informed of developments.'

'I'll see you to the door,' Elise murmured as Kyle went on ahead of his father. 'We have to talk.'

'Are you okay?' Mark asked her, putting a gentle hand under her chin. 'You're very pale.'

'And your hands are cold,' she countered. 'Sorry, that was rude . . . I'm fine.'

'I told you not to get involved if anything happened.'

'I couldn't leave Joan out there on her own and I was worried about Angelique.'

'That was no reason to go charging up the lane without a thought for your own safety. Supposing there had been a troublemaker on the loose? Thank goodness Joan had the sense to call the police first. What a night.'

'What do you think Kyle and Angie were really up to?'

'Well I believe them when they say nothing happened. I don't think their friendship is any more than student related. Kyle doesn't fib and I'm sure Angie is equally as honest. They were probably talking and forgot the time and hoped they'd get away with it. Unfortunately, events conspired against them.'

Only her sense of pride stopped Elise from sagging against Mark in relief. His words provided the reassurances she craved and although she was more than capable of looking after herself, it was comforting to have a reliable male slant.

'Get some rest,' Mark insisted, 'for what's left of the night.'

'You too,' Elise replied.

'Come on, Dad. It's cold out here,' Kyle called out from the car park. 'Some of us have to get up in the morning.'

'Coming,' he called back. 'By the

way,' Mark asked, 'are we still on for that date at the fairground, or have you decided the Hampson men are not people with whom you want to share your candy floss?'

Elise found herself being drawn into the magnetism of Mark's tired smile. 'As long as you can face being seen on the helter skelter with me.'

'There are some sacrifices to dignity I suppose a man must make.' His lips brushed Elise's. 'Promise me you'll all take care? I don't know what's going on here but I won't rest easy until I find out who's behind all this. I'll be in touch.'

When she went back into the kitchen, Joan was clearing away the tea things. 'I don't like this at all,' Joan said. 'I mean why pick on us?'

'Do you want to spend the night in the flat with us?' Elise asked, bearing Mark's warning in mind. 'Just in case someone is hanging about outside.'

Joan's reply was a robust, 'I'd like to see them try anything! If they come back I'll be more than ready for them!'

'You know you should be grateful to me and Kyle,' Angie said. 'If we hadn't been out late you wouldn't have known someone had let the donkeys loose.'

'You can't argue with that one,' Joan laughed and kissed her granddaughter's cheek, 'but don't ever do anything like that again. I might have been a bit of a tearaway in my youth but I won't have you upsetting Elise.'

'Sorry, Gran,' Angie looked suitably stricken. 'It was only a meeting about the demonstration. Kyle's had this brilliant idea.'

'Which we can all hear about another time. Now, Angelique, bed,' Elise ordered.

★   ★   ★

'Mrs Trent?' Gary approached Joan the next morning.

'Hello, Gary, what can I do for you?'

'I heard about all the trouble last night.'

'I should think all of Beech Mead knows about it by now,' Joan replied.

'I don't want you to think I'm speaking out of turn, but . . . '

'Do you know something?' Joan stopped pricing melons.

'It's Kyle and Angie . . . They have been getting very close.'

'They're co-ordinating the college action group, aren't they?'

'It's more than that. I mean Angie's buzzing.'

'She's what?'

'You know, making things happen.'

Joan took a deep breath. Gary was never articulate at the best of times and it was like getting blood out of a stone to try to understand what he was saying.

'Are you telling me that Angie is responsible for painting slogans on the clubhouse wall?'

'I dunno really . . . ' Gary shuffled his feet and began to look as though he wished he hadn't started the conversation. 'I don't want to make trouble.'

'No one is in trouble,' Joan said, 'but if you know something then you should go to the police.'

'Don't wanna do that.' Gary was now backing out of the shop. 'Forget I said anything.'

After he'd gone Joan continued pricing the melons, glad there were no visits scheduled for the day. She didn't think she was up to coping should there be any more dramas with the animals.

So far Mrs Newman hadn't carried through her threat to complain to the authorities, but Joan was not optimistic that she would let the matter rest.

Maureen scuttled in from the store-room. 'Sorry, got held up with the milkman. He wanted to know what happened with the donkeys. Rumours are flying round all over the place. Did I see Gary talking to you?'

'Did you or Harry see anything last night?' Joan asked. 'I mean, I know you don't live on the premises, but Harry likes to keep an eye on things, doesn't he?'

'No, I don't think so,' Maureen began to look equally as evasive as her son.

Joan frowned. 'Are you covering up?' she asked, aware that Maureen's reply had been as ambiguous as her son's.

'Whatever gave you that idea?' Maureen attempted to lighten the atmosphere.

'Not what — who,' Joan said rather sharply. 'Your son, Gary.'

'What's he been saying?' Maureen demanded.

'He suggested that Angie was responsible for daubing that slogan in the clubhouse.'

'No!' Maureen now looked shocked.

'That's what I thought, but Gary says she and Kyle have been stirring things up with this action group.'

'I hate to speak against my own son,' Maureen said in a quiet voice, 'but I think he's attracted to Angie and, well, his feelings aren't reciprocated.'

'You're saying he made up this story about Angie out of spite? That doesn't sound like Gary.'

'It doesn't, does it?' Maureen agreed. 'But what other explanation can there be? You've seen the way he moons after her. I'm not saying anything against Angie; she's a lovely girl, but my Gary's a bit of an introvert and he might sense a rebuff if he thought she was getting close to Kyle.'

'You surely don't think he's responsible for what happened last night?'

'No!' Maureen was firm on that one. 'Whatever else he is, Gary wouldn't harm any of the animals — and to be honest I think he would be too scared to break into the clubhouse and start playing around with paint.'

'I agree with you,' Joan replied. 'Look, I'll have a word with Angie on her own and see if she and Kyle can downgrade their protest. Don't mention any of this to Elise will you? She's got enough on her plate at the moment.'

'I won't.' Maureen looked relieved that Joan wasn't going to take things further.

'You know Beech Mead used to be

such a quiet place. Nothing much ever happened here. Now we've got protests, planning applications . . . '

'And your engagement,' Maureen put in.

'I'd almost overlooked that,' Joan admitted with a laugh. 'Seth's been so busy I've not seen much of him recently.'

'Have you settled on a date?' Maureen asked.

'Not yet, maybe in the summer. I'd really like to get things straight before then. Don't worry,' she smiled encouragingly, 'you'll be the first to know.' Joan glanced up at the clock. 'Heavens, is that the time? The morning's nearly gone and we haven't done anything. Can I leave serving in the shop to you, Maureen? There are some calls I simply have to make.'

Joan bustled towards the office. First and foremost she had a business to run. All other issues would have to take a back seat she decided as she picked up the telephone to return the first of a long list of calls.

6

Seth Baxter greeted Elise and Mark as they approached the village hall. 'Hello there. Quite a turn out wouldn't you say?'

The forecourt was a seething mass of bodies. A group of protestors was waving banners and there was some heckling of the officials as they arrived, but Elise was relieved to see that most of the students had joined the meeting in an orderly manner in order to hear what the developers had to say.

'I was expecting more of a show-down,' Elise admitted, still feeling nervous. Angie had assured her that the rally would be peaceful but they both knew from previous experiences of other demonstrations that if a rogue element infiltrated them then things could turn nasty.

'Our lot have made sure there'll be

none of that,' Mark assured Elise with a squeeze of her fingers. 'They'll be keeping a careful look out for known agitators.'

Several uniformed officers were keeping a discreet eye on the proceedings. Most of them were relaxed and exchanged friendly banter with the group of young people outside.

'Joan's inside if you want her,' Seth said. 'She's been helping with refreshments. I don't think they expected quite such a healthy turnout and there's been a call for reinforcements.'

'We'd better get inside as well then and see what it's all about, hadn't we? Catch up with you later, Seth,' Mark said.

With a friendly wave Seth sauntered off towards a group of his cricketing friends who were enjoying the evening air outside the village hall.

'Goodness, what a crush,' Elise said as they pushed open the door.

Several efficient looking public relations assistants were greeting newcomers, handing out glossy brochures and directing people to the fast diminishing number of free seats available.

'I think I'll stand at the back,' Mark informed Elise. 'That way I can keep a better eye on things should there be any unrest or awkward questions.'

'I'll see if Joan needs any help,' Elise replied as she began to forge her way through the crowded hall towards the kitchen at the back. She hadn't got very far before a sharp whistling noise from the on stage microphone alerted Elise's attention to the fact that the meeting was about to begin. Flattening herself against the wall, she decided to stay where she was as she waited for the chairperson to speak.

There was a row of seats on the stage and the panel seemed to be comprised of equal numbers of men and women. Elise noted the mix, as well as the diverse age range, with approval.

'Good evening, ladies and gentleman,' a suited official began. He then went on to introduce himself and the various other representatives of the development company. As he outlined his company's plans for the proposed caravan park, Elise was surprised to discover the developers were a respectable, forward thinking company with a strong social conscience and an awareness of green issues. The spokesman went on to insist the development would in no way detract from the surrounding natural beauty or the environment of the area.

'We envisage using the park as a promotion for holiday lets for people such as bird watchers, environmentalists, those with a genuine enthusiasm for the countryside. People who want to maintain its natural beauty. Now,' he finished up with a smile, 'I'm sure you've heard enough from me. It's time for questions from the floor, which I and my colleagues will attempt to answer as honestly as we can.'

The half hour session overran until the chairperson put a halt to the proceedings by suggesting they break for refreshments. The crush in the church hall showed no signs of abating. Everyone had stayed to hear exactly what was going on and there were still several hands raised from potential questioners.

'I'll leave you to socialise and if any of you have further cause for concern, then please come and speak to me personally. I appreciate the stand our young friends have made outside and I think it goes to prove that Beech Mead is the sort of community that cares about its future, as we all do. We intend to encourage healthy criticism and we also plan to consult the next generation regarding any new proposals.'

The round of applause that greeted his words was more than a polite acknowledgement of his speech and the buzz of conversation afterwards was positive as everyone surged forward to speak to various members of the panel.

'Hello.' Elise felt a tap on her shoulder. 'I don't believe we've met.' She recognised the man behind her as the spokesperson for the developers.

'Chris Saunders, chief public relations officer.'

'Elise Trent.'

'Nice to meet you, Elise.' He smiled as they shook hands. 'Do you have a specific interest in the project or are you here to look at the plans and see what's going on?'

'A bit of both really. My mother-in-law is Joan Trent. She runs the farm shop that backs onto Merritt's Wood. Your company has been in touch with her.'

'Of course,' Chris nodded. 'I thought the name was familiar. You're French, aren't you?'

'Yes, but I've lived here for many years. I think I should also tell you that my daughter Angelique is one of the ringleaders organising the demonstration outside.'

'I approve of youngsters with a social conscience,' Chris replied, 'so no issues there,' he said with an easy smile. 'Is there anything you'd like to discuss with me?' he asked.

'I am not directly involved with the proposal, but Joan is in two minds about what to do. Have you spoken to her yet this evening?' she asked.

Chris made a face. 'I tried but there's this extremely efficient lady in the kitchen brandishing tea pots and milk cartons with frightening ferocity. She wouldn't let me near the place. Said I was a health hazard or something, and as I wasn't wearing the obligatory white overall she sent me smartly on my way.'

Elise laughed. 'Now that sounds like Mrs Newman.'

'Councillor Newman's wife?'

'That's the one.'

'She's a bit scary, isn't she?'

'We had a bit of a set-to with her regarding our goat,' Elise confessed. 'I would tell you about it but it's a long story and I don't think this is the right time.'

'In that case,' Chris waved to someone in a far corner of the room, 'would you join me for dinner one evening when we can talk properly without constant interruptions?'

The invitation took Elise more than a little by surprise. 'Er, yes. That would be lovely.'

'Excellent, I'll be in touch. If you'll excuse me?'

'Of course.'

Elise watched him cross the room to where another suited official was trying to gain his attention. There was no denying Chris Saunders was a very attractive man. Elise realised of course that being in public relations he would be socially at ease on these sorts of occasions, but all the same his concern for the village seemed genuine and Elise respected that.

'There you are.' A red-faced Joan emerged from the kitchen. 'Who was that? I missed the presentation.'

'Chris Saunders, he's with the development company.'

'Did I hear him asking you out to dinner?'

'You don't mind do you?'

'It's none of my business, Elise, but what about Mark?'

'Mark and I are not an item.' Elise tilted her chin at Joan. 'I'm free to go out with whosoever I want to.'

'Of course,' Joan agreed hurriedly. 'Actually it might be a good idea for you to go out with him. I'll give you a list of questions I would've liked to ask him, then if the conversation flags you'll have something to talk about.'

'Why don't you come along too?' Elise suggested.

Joan gave her an old-fashioned look. 'I don't think a mother-in-law was part of the remit, do you?'

'Probably not,' Elise agreed, a small part of her already beginning to regret taking up the invitation.

Joan changed the subject. 'I have some news for you,' she said. 'While I was closeted in the kitchen with Mrs Newman that husband of hers poked his head round the door. He assures me that his son has recovered from the trauma of being head-butted by Gertie and that the matter will go no further.'

'That is a relief.'

'Isn't it? Actually,' Joan lowered her voice, 'he also confided in me that his wife spoils the child outrageously and in his personal opinion being got at by a goat would have done the boy a power of good. Luckily his wife didn't overhear the exchange, but we're all friends again which is a great weight off my mind.'

'What does the councillor think of the planning proposal?' Elise asked.

'He feels it'll bring prosperity to the area and will be giving it his full support. Winners all round, wouldn't you say?'

'Have you decided what you're going to do?'

'Not yet,' Joan replied, 'but there's going to be a subcommittee meeting. I'll go to that and see how everyone feels.'

'What do we do now?' Elise looked round. The meeting showed no sign of thinning out.

'It's such a crush in here and I don't know about you, but after the heat of the kitchen I think I'd like to go home. Have you seen Seth?'

'He was outside when Mark and I arrived.'

'I'd better go have a word with him, then I think I'll be off.'

'I'll go and look for Angie,' Elise said. 'I'm glad the demonstration was peaceful.' The light was going from the day as Elise emerged from the church hall.

'Mum,' Angie called over. 'Is it okay with you if I go to the burger bar? I'm starving.'

'Why do you always have to eat those things?' Elise demanded. 'They're not good for you.'

'I eat healthily during the week, you see to that. Chips every now and then can't be that bad.'

'Please, Elise.' Kyle appeared at her side. 'We won't be late, I promise. Besides,' he added with what bordered on a sly smile, 'didn't I hear you and Dad making plans to eat candy floss and toffee apples?'

'How healthy is that? As for riding down the helter skelter . . . dignity, Mum?'

Angie's expression was so false innocence that Elise wanted to burst out laughing. Her daughter was infuriating and far too strong-minded for her own good — and Elise loved her to bits.

'Go on with you then.' She restrained the impulse to kiss her daughter and embarrass her in front of her friends who were all grinning impishly at her. 'Here,' she delved into her bag and produced some money. 'Treat yourselves.'

'Cool — thanks, Mum!'

With an airy wave of her fingers Angie strolled off with her friends, all chatting nineteen-to-the-dozen.

'Did I just see you giving my son some money?' Mark asked.

'It was actually intended for my daughter,' Elise replied.

'Never trust a Hampson when there's

money on offer,' he joked. 'So, was my son right?'

'Sorry?'

'Do we have a date tonight?'

'Things run in threes, don't they?' Elise replied.

'I don't understand.'

'Seth and Joan are off somewhere. Angie's out with your son and her friends, so let's go for it, too.'

'I was actually hoping you'd accept my invitation because you found my charm irresistible, but being the best of three will have to do, I suppose,' Mark acknowledged with a smile. 'Now what are you in the mood for? Traditional English, French, Indian, Thai or Chinese? I can offer them all.'

'I think I'd like The Bistro, actually.'

'Good choice. Shall we?' Mark held out his arm in a gesture of courtesy and after saying goodbye to one or two colleagues who were still lingering outside the church hall, they made their way to his car.

* ★ *

'What did you think of the meeting?' Mark asked after they'd ordered their meal.

'Chris Saunders spoke well. I was actually impressed.'

'I was pleased things were fairly ordered outside as well.' Mark buttered a bread roll. 'I have to hand it to Angie, she stopped any nonsense.'

'Nonsense?' Elise felt a flutter of alarm.

'One or two of the boys wanted to be a bit silly about things but she soon put them down.'

Elise was debating whether or not to tell Mark about Chris's dinner invitation but before she could say anything, he changed the subject.

'By the way, Jacques Dubois . . . remember him?'

'The disappearing Frenchman? Have you found him?'

Mark shook his head. 'We checked up with his car hire company but the booking was made in the name of an antiques company which proves not to exist.'

'He seemed so normal,' Elise said in surprise, 'although now I come to think about it when I said I came from the Alpes-Maritimes, he got rather, how do you say in English, edgy?'

Mark nodded. 'You know, when I moved out from the smoke and into the country I thought life would be nice and quiet. Instead we've got property developers and protests, fake Frenchman and,' he paused, 'I met you!' Mark held up a hand. 'It's alright, I'm not about to ask you to marry me again. I know the score on that one.'

'Mark, I . . . '

He shook his head. 'It's all right. I can do grown up. Now, if you've finished we'd better be getting back. Having taken Kyle to task for being late, I don't want to find he's standing at the door of the flat waiting for me to let him in.'

'He's still staying with you?' Elise asked.

'I knew there was something else I had to tell you . . . it's permanent for the time being. Amanda my ex-wife is getting married again.'

'Really?'

'I've met him and have no issues. After the ceremony she'll be moving in with him, so she's in the throes of selling up house too. It's all a bit disruptive for Kyle, so he's staying with me on a semi permanent basis until things get fixed up. I'm still house hunting but these things take time . . . ' Aware that she wasn't paying much attention to what he was saying as they drove into the car park of the farm shop, Mark prompted with, 'Elise?'

She grabbed Mark's arm causing him to swerve.

'Steady. What's the matter?'

'Look.' She pointed through the window.

'I don't see anything.'

'There in the clubhouse. There's a light on.'

'What?'

'They're back!'

'Whoever they are, this time I'm determined to put a stop to things,' Mark said as he killed the engine, jumped out of the car and sped toward the cricket pitch, Elise running after him.

7

The snapping of a twig under Elise's shoe sounded as loud as gunfire in the quiet night air.

'Ssh,' Mark put a finger to his lips.

'Sorry. Can you see anything?' Elise whispered.

'There's someone in there and I intend to catch them red handed,' Mark hissed.

'Red paint handed,' Elise sniggered, then put a hand over her mouth as Mark glared at her in the darkness. 'Sorry. Nerves.' She slipped a hand into Mark's.

Until now as a single parent for over ten years she had been an independent woman, but being with Mark was reassuring, a male quality she enjoyed.

'Do be careful,' she urged him, colliding with his broad back as he came to an unexpected halt.

'I will.' He crept towards the door of the clubhouse.

'We've got the advantage of surprise on our side,' he murmured. 'Now don't say anything. We're going for it.'

The next moment he pushed open the door. Elise half expected him to shout out, 'Freeze!', but instead he strode into the clubhouse.

'Police,' he announced. 'Don't anyone move.'

Elise cannoned into his back for the second time that evening as he came to another sudden halt just in front of her.

'Harry?' she gasped peering round Mark's bulk. 'Maureen? What on earth are you doing?'

★   ★   ★

'I can't believe it.' Joan and Seth stared at Elise as she updated them on the evening's events.

They were all seated in Joan's cottage after Mark had taken the Jenkins off to the police station.

'Apparently they were both worried about their jobs,' Elise said. 'They didn't want to damage anything. They were trying to make the development an unattractive prospect I suppose.'

'That explains why that bit of turf they cut from the pitch was such a neat job,' Seth put in. 'I wondered about that at the time. I suppose Harry couldn't bring himself to do any proper damage to the wicket.'

'What were they going to do this time?' Joan asked.

'We never got round to that,' Elise replied. 'They thought everyone was out because they heard me making plans to go out to dinner with Mark outside the church hall, and they knew you and Seth weren't here and Angie had gone off with her friends. That left the coast clear.'

'They had everything neatly planned. I'll say that for them,' Joan agreed. 'I'm glad it was them, if you know what I mean.'

'And I'm glad that lets me and Kyle

off the hook,' Angie said.

She had catapulted into the club-house in the middle of all the drama, brandishing a golf stick that she had found abandoned outside the shop.

Like Mark and Elise, she and Kyle had come home and seen the lights on and were trying to decide what to do when they heard Mark's raised voice. Fearing he might be in trouble they had grabbed up the first weapon that came to hand and headed across the cricket pitch.

'I'm sorry, darling,' Elise apologised to her daughter. 'You know I never really suspected you.'

'All the same,' Angie said, 'things were a bit uncomfortable for Kyle and me, what with us arranging the protest and all.'

'Yes, but you would never harm any of the animals and they could have hurt themselves running up and down the lane.'

'I thought Maureen loved the animals as much as we do,' Angie shook her head. 'I can't believe she let them out.'

'Yes, I would never have suspected her of hurting the donkeys either,' Elise agreed.

Joan cleared her throat. 'Actually,' she said quietly, 'I've a bit of a confession to make.'

'Don't tell me you were responsible for letting the donkeys out?' Seth's bushy eyebrows rose in surprise.

'Not as such, but I have discovered that one of the donkeys can actually nudge the gate open with her nose. I think she sensed all the disturbance in the clubhouse and probably wanted to find out what was going on and that's what happened the night Kyle was hiding in the bushes.'

'I can't wait to see the expression on Kyle's face when I tell him he was being stalked by a donkey and forced to hide in the undergrowth!' Angie broke into peals of laughter. 'His street cred will sink like a stone!'

'You mustn't do that,' Elise reproached her.

'Why not? Sometimes he gets too big

for his boots. It would serve him right if I had accepted Gary's invitation to that gig.'

'What gig?' Elise demanded.

'It's okay, Mum. I turned him down. Actually he's been a bit off about it ever since.'

'I wonder . . . ' Joan said slowly.

'More confessions?' Seth asked.

'What if he suspected what his parents were up to and that was why he suggested Angie and Kyle were responsible?'

'He put the blame on me?' Angie's voice was now a squawk of protest. 'The zit!'

'Angie, dear, language,' Elise reprimanded her.

'That's exactly what he is — a pimple.'

'It's only my suspicion,' Joan said. 'We don't know anything for sure but it would explain things, wouldn't it? What's going to happen to Maureen and Harry now?' she asked.

'I suppose it depends on whether or

not the cricket club want to prosecute,' Seth replied. 'I should imagine they would like the whole thing hushed up and if what you say is true about the donkeys, well they weren't responsible, and as no harm was done to your premises, they may just get off with some sort of official warning.'

'I do hope so,' Joan said. 'I don't want to take things further. Actually in a way I can sympathise with Maureen. It's been an unsettling time for us all.'

'Us protesters have to stick together, don't we Gran? I can do you a cool banner if you want to join our numbers. Although strictly speaking I suppose it won't be necessary now.'

Angie and Joan high-fived, leaving Seth and Elise to exchange tolerant glances.

'I hope your coming into the family will be a stabilising influence on my mother-in-law and my daughter,' Elise said to Seth with a smile.

'At the risk of letting the side down, Elise,' he confided, 'I'm rather with

116

them on this one. Don't worry, I'm not going to turn into a hippy, but I do believe in standing up for people's rights.'

'Yay, three against one, Mum!' Angie now slapped her palm against Seth's.

'Really,' Elise tutted, but her glare didn't really work and she found herself laughing with the rest of them.

'Say, have you thought any more about a date?' Angie asked Joan and Seth. 'All my friends think it's cool, you two getting married. If there's a party they want an invite.'

'We haven't actually got as far as that,' Joan replied. 'Of course we'll have some sort of celebration. The church hall would be a good place. There are so many people we want to invite. I think we'll have to hold a party after we get married.'

'If we make it in the summer then the guests can all spill outside,' Seth agreed. 'The ladies who do the cricket club teas can put on a bit of a show for us.'

'It's going to be the social event of the summer,' Angie laughed delightedly. 'I'll arrange the music, shall I?'

'Nothing too loud, dear, please.'

'Don't worry. I'll trawl the archives for all the sixties stuff. You'd like that, wouldn't you?'

'I've always enjoyed a bit of old-fashioned dancing,' Seth said. 'You know, the type where you actually hold your lady in your arms?'

'Me too, Seth,' Angie agreed with him.

'Don't tell me my modern, rebellious daughter has a romantic streak in her?' Elise joked.

'Before things get totally out of hand,' Joan stopped them all, 'I suggest we discuss everything at a later date. I don't know about you, but I intend on going to bed. In case you hadn't noticed it's gone midnight and over the past month we seem to have had more than our fill of late nights. We've got jobs to go to in the morning.'

'I haven't,' Seth pointed out, 'but for

the sake of unity I can take a hint. By the way,' he said as he stood up, 'it was a good meeting don't you think?'

'Chris Saunders has asked Elise out to dinner,' Joan replied.

'Hey, Mum, do I get to give the lecture now? You know the one about staying out late and not doing anything silly?'

Elise stifled her irritation with Joan. She would have preferred to break the news to her daughter in her own time and on a more appropriate occasion.

'Chris is new to the area,' she began to explain. 'I think he wants to know how the locals really feel about the development and he probably thought a relaxed atmosphere was best.'

'What about Mark?' Angie demanded. 'Does he know about this date?'

'I haven't told him.'

'Then you should . . . ' Angie said earnestly.

'I will,' Elise replied. 'But for now Joan is right. It's time we were all in bed.'

' . . . before he finds out about it from someone else.'

'Angelique, bed,' Elise said firmly. 'Thanks, Joan,' she called over her shoulder with a hint of sarcasm.

★ ★ ★

'Call for you, Mum,' Angie shouted up the stairs as Elise emerged from the shower.

'At this time of the morning? Who is it?' She took the phone.

'Chris Saunders here. Sorry to call so early but I'll be away for a few days, so I'm afraid I'm going to have to postpone our dinner date until I get back. I'm moving house and as usual there are problems.'

'That's quite all right,' Elise said in relief. 'I understand.'

'Good. I've got my diary in front of me. May I suggest next weekend? Are you free on Saturday?'

'Er . . . ' Elise hunted round for a notepad and pencil, ' . . . yes, that should be fine,' she said, unable to find one and hoping she would remember to write the details down.

'Excellent. I'll call for you at the shop about seven?'

'Could I suggest that we make it lunch?' Elise said.

'If you would prefer,' Chris agreed. 'Lunchtime it is.'

The phone rang again almost immediately Elise hung up.

'Mark?' Elise hoped she was right this time.

'It's only me,' the principal of the language college said straight away. 'Can you come in today? We've got a whole new batch of application forms and I really could do with an extra pair of hands and I've also got a video telephone link up with my French counterpart scheduled for ten o'clock and you know how badly I speak your language.'

'Of course,' Elise replied with a laugh. 'I'll be with you in an hour's time if that's all right?'

'Any time you like.'

Elise towel-dried her hair as she went back into the bedroom. She could hear the radio playing in the kitchen and the smell of toast wafting up the stairs.

'Make me a slice,' she called out to Angie. 'I'll give you a lift this morning if you like. I've got to go into work.'

'So do you have a hot date?' Angie asked over breakfast. 'I must say he's keen.'

'He's moving house,' Elise began, desperately trying to remember his message. It was always the same if she didn't write things down immediately.

Just then the phone rang yet again. 'What is it with that telephone this morning?' Elise demanded.

'Hi? Gosh Mum's popular this morning,' Angie said. 'You're the third man who's phoned. You'll have to take your place in the queue. I don't suppose you want to talk to me instead?' After a few more pleasantries she handed over the receiver.

'Who is it?'

'Mark,' she mouthed before sauntering out of the kitchen.

'What was all that about three men?' Mark demanded.

'Take no notice,' Elise replied. 'Have you any news?'

'I'm sure you'll be pleased to hear that the charges against Harry and Maureen will be dropped. The cricket club decided there was no point in pursuing things and Joan's said pretty much the same.'

'That's wonderful news.'

'I've got an even better bit of news,' Mark added. 'The fair is in town this weekend, so are you still on for that candy floss and a ride on the big wheel?'

'I'll look forward to it,' Elise laughed. 'And now I really must go. Angie's waiting for a lift.'

'In that case see you at the weekend. Bye.'

It was only as Elise was driving along after dropping Angie off that she realised she'd still not written down Chris's message.

8

The tinny music of the galloper drifted down the hill as the four of them trudged to the top to look at the view.

'Why do fairgrounds always smell of hot toffee and onions?' Mark demanded.

'Because that's what they do, Dad,' Kyle explained to his father in patient tones. 'They make burgers and toffee apples and I want one.'

'Really, Kyle, you sound like a six-year-old child,' his father repri-manded him.

'Lucky you.' Angie cast a sideways glance at Elise, 'I'm not allowed to eat things like that. Mum says they're bad for me.'

'Well if you're looking for healthy eating today, Elise,' Mark sympathised, 'you're going to be out of luck and hungry. It's strictly candy floss, toffee apples, and hot dogs with fried onions and tomato sauce.'

Angie clapped her hands. 'You wouldn't want me to starve now, Mum, would you?' She batted her mascara-laden eyelashes at her mother. 'You're always telling me how important it is to eat regularly.'

'Why am I always painted as the villain of the piece?' Elise puffed as they reached the summit. 'Look at that.'

She pointed to the scene that met her eyes. The attraction was throbbing with visitors and the usual cacophony associated with a vibrant fairground. Huge shire horses trudged backwards and forwards in the shafts of brightly coloured gypsy caravans, decorated with all the tools of their trade.

A huge big dipper scarred the skyline and excited shrieks rent the air as the on board riders — clinging onto the coaches for dear life — were plunged downwards into a spray of cold water.

'Come on, Kyle,' Angie dragged on his arm, 'let's see if we can bag a plastic duck on the shooting range.'

'Bet I pop one before you.' Kyle took up the challenge.

'Meet you back at the fortune telling tent by four o'clock,' Mark called after them. 'Got your mobiles on?'

'Chill, Dad,' Kyle called back. 'Everything's fine.'

'So,' Elise smiled up at him, 'that leaves you and me. Are you on for the helter skelter or would it offend your dignity?'

'It would, but in the name of community relations I'm prepared to give it a go. Come on.'

It was Mark who now held Elise's hand as they made their way towards the stands. The queue for the helter skelter was a long one and they passed their time laughing at the antics of a clown and his small dog. He was followed by a one man band who clashed cymbals between his knees, blew on a mouth organ and sang songs very badly. Elise laughed so much there were tears in her eyes by the time he'd finished.

'Did you ever hear anything so terrible?' she asked.

'I have to admit, not often,' Mark replied. 'Do you have fairs like this in France?'

'We do,' Elise said, 'but this one seems different somehow. I know the origins are middle European but here everything somehow seems so English.'

'It's because it's by the sea, I suppose.'

'What has that to do with it?' Elise asked, looking confused.

'It sort of reminds you that Europe's that-a-way,' Mark pointed over her head. 'I don't know. It's not my day for sophisticated thinking.'

He grinned down at her, the smile tugging at the corner of his mouth and Elise experienced an absurd urge for him to kiss her. There had been no more shared intimacies of that nature since the day she had turned down his proposal. Although Elise was grateful for his continued friendship she began to realise that her own feelings were beginning to change towards Mark.

He was always there for her in the same way that Kyle accepted it was his duty to look after Angie in a manner that must be considered as old-fashioned courtesy to the young.

Was this what love felt like second time around? Elise did not know. She'd been so young when she had met Peter. Sometimes it was difficult to remember the early days.

She was no longer a carefree student. Now she was a woman of forty with a daughter who was fast growing up. She supposed her emotions would be very different from those of the young girl of twenty who had fallen in love with a poor English artist.

'Look out, we're on!' Mark nudged Elise. 'Move yourself.'

Clutching their mats together they climbed up the steps and paused at the top.

'You'd better go first,' Mark said, 'it's been a while since I've done this sort of thing. I'm not as flexible as I used to be.'

Wriggling herself into a seated position, Elise pushed off down the slide. She could hear Mark muttering behind her as, like a child, she broke into exhilarated laughter and landed in an inelegant heap at the bottom of the chute. Moments later Mark's body was wrapped around hers.

'Sorry, my mat didn't have a brake,' he apologised as their legs became entangled and amused bystanders helped to sort them out. 'You should signal before you stop. I may have to book you, Madam, for not observing the rules of the skelter.'

The feel of his body against hers left Elise with a heady sensation she couldn't identify.

Until now she had never realised just how attractive a man Mark was. Oh, he was good looking, yes, but she'd always seen their friendship first and foremost. But now she noticed several of the women in the queue flirtily eyeing him as they leapt to his aid first before asking if she was all right.

'Where to next?' he asked as they finally disposed of their mats and had brushed each other down.

'Let's do the big wheel,' Elise suggested. 'It's such a clear day we'll be able to see for miles.'

The queue for the big wheel was even longer than that for the helter skelter. This time two acrobats entertained them, entwining their bodies into impossible poses, smiling all the time at the look of incredulity on the faces of the fair goers.

'I don't think I'll be trying that one,' Mark said as one of the acrobats inverted himself. 'That looks extremely uncomfortable and I'm not sure I'd know how to get out of it.'

As the operator closed the restraint across their laps, their little carriage lurched forwards, then slowly upwards.

'I love this view over the South Downs,' Elise said as they steadily rose higher and higher.

'You know the South Downs Way goes from Eastbourne all the way to the border with Hampshire? I'd to do a geography course as part of my induction to the area,' Mark said.

'You walked all the way?' Elise gave him a surprised look.

'It's about eighty five miles long!' Mark replied. 'So no, I didn't, but I did bits of it. You'd be amazed what you can see; evidence of Roman settlements, flint mines, barrows — and the wildlife is something else too. Wild orchids and wheatears and we saw several deer. Of course they were very timid so we couldn't get close to them.'

'It sounds lovely.'

'If you like we could make that our next outing, not the full eighty miles of course.'

'I'm pleased to hear it,' Elise laughed as she shaded her eyes against the sun.

'Twenty would be manageable in a day, wouldn't you say?'

'No, I would not,' Elise protested. 'You English are far too fond of the fresh air and my feet would not like such an outing.'

'Only joking.' Mark draped a casual arm round her shoulders. 'We're nearly at the top. What can you see? Ow!' he added. 'Do you have to squeeze my hand quite so hard?'

'Look! Down there — there by the helter skelter — and it's not what, it's who.'

'Who?' Mark repeated in confusion.

'The man who pretended to be Jacques Dubois! It's him!'

'Are you sure?' Mark no longer sounded playful.

'I'd recognise him anywhere. He's talking to another man.'

'You're right,' Mark agreed slapping the bar of their seat in frustration. 'How long does it take to get back to the ground in this thing? Keep your eyes fixed on him, Elise, and I'll try to raise a signal on my mobile.'

He pressed a few buttons. 'It's no good,' he announced in exasperation a few moments later. 'There's too much else going on round here.'

'He's still there. I don't know what he's up to but he's looking very furtive . . . bother. There's a tent in the way. I can't see him.'

'Never mind, we're nearly at ground level again. Get ready to move the moment he opens us up.'

'Hey, steady on, mate,' the operator complained as Mark and Elise leapt out of their seat and began racing through the long grass towards the helter skelter.

'I can't see him.' Elise arrived first.

'What about the man he was talking to? Would you recognise him?' Mark asked hopefully.

'No. There are so many people, it's impossible to tell.' Elise looked round in frustration. 'I didn't imagine it, did I?'

'I saw him too,' Mark reminded her. 'Excuse me.' He stopped a passing worker. 'Who runs the helter skelter?'

The youth shifted nervously, his natural antipathy towards authority kicking in. 'What's it to you?' he demanded.

'I need to know. It's important.'

'Sorry, can't help you,' the boy said and loped off before Mark could question him further.

Several other enquiries gave the same negative response.

'This is hopeless,' Elise said, frustrated. 'They know you're a policeman.'

'You're probably right. Let's round up Kyle and Angie. I'm sorry, Elise, we're going to have to cut our day out short.'

'What do you think the so called Jacques Dubois was doing?'

'I should imagine a fairground is an ideal place to make contact with someone. I'm not saying the fairground is involved in any way but it's the sort of place where you can melt into the crowd at a moment's notice. Come on, let's find the others.'

It was another full hour before they finally caught Kyle coming out of the hall of mirrors. Angie was clinging onto

Kyle, laughing at the outrageous reflections they'd seen inside.

'Hello?' Kyle looked up at Mark as he strode over to the pair of them. 'We're not late are we? You said four o'clock and it's only half past two, or has my watch stopped?'

'Sorry, we're going to have to leave.'

'Mum?' Angie was all concern now, all signs of amusement wiped from her face. 'What's wrong? You're not ill, are you?'

'No, nothing like that. We think we spotted Jacques Dubois.'

'Who's he?' Kyle asked looking perplexed.

'It's a long story. We'll tell you about it in the car.'

★ ★ ★

'You mean this was the man whose wallet you found in your bag?' Angie asked as they sped back to Beech Mead. 'The one there was all the trouble about?'

135

'I think so,' Elise admitted reluctantly.

'You don't sound very sure.'

'I'm beginning to wonder if I did see him now,' she said. 'I thought it was him but there was no sign of him later.'

'If he is back in the area it could mean they're planning another operation,' Mark said. 'I'm afraid I'm going to have to drop you all off at the farm shop. Elise, can you run Kyle home?'

'No need,' Kyle replied, 'I'll walk. Maybe I'll go into town see what's happening on the local scene.'

'No staying out late,' Mark said with a warning look at his son as they drew into the forecourt of the farm shop. 'Who's that?' he added.

'Chris Saunders,' Angie said. 'He's the publicity guy from the property developers.'

'What's he doing here?' Mark demanded.

With a sinking heart Elise remembered today was the day she was supposed to be meeting up with him for their date.

'He's got a date with Mum. You didn't forget, did you?' Angie asked looking at Elise.

That was exactly what had happened, Elise thought as she tried to find the right words to frame her explanation to Mark.

'I must say he's a bit early,' Angie said.

'I'm sorry I should have mentioned it earlier,' Elise said to Mark, 'but Angelique is right; it slipped my mind.'

'There's no reason why you should tell me your every move.' There was no answering smile in Mark's eyes. 'You're perfectly free to go out with whomsoever you wish. I must go. Kyle, don't be late home.'

'Hello.' Chris hurried over to them, the expression on his face uncertain. 'Did I get the date wrong? I've been waiting for ages. I didn't want to miss you and the lady in the shop said she didn't know where you were. We did say lunch not dinner, didn't we?'

'Yes, I'm so sorry,' Elise apologised

as, with a spurt of gravel, Mark turned his car round and drove quickly out of the forecourt leaving the four of them choking in the dust created by the sharp manoeuvre of his wheels.

9

Elise suggested that everyone go inside. 'I could make us a meal as we all missed out on lunch. Kyle, you're invited, too, of course,' she said.

'If you're sure?' Kyle looked at little uncomfortable. 'I wouldn't want to intrude.'

'Mum's the best cook in the world,' Angie said, 'so you'd best stay. That way,' she murmured in an aside that wasn't quite out of Elise's earshot, 'you can keep an eye on Chris and Mum if you want to save her relationship with your father.'

Before Elise could reprimand her daughter the pair of them were huddled together discussing their plans.

'Why don't you go and find Joan as well, Angelique?' Elise raised her voice. 'If I know her she probably only had a scratch lunch, if anything to eat at all.'

'This is most kind of you, Elise.' Chris looked much happier now the arrangement had been confirmed. 'Actually it will be a good idea to speak to you all together. I have lots of plans to show you and discuss.'

'There you are.' Maureen looked relieved as they all trooped into the shop. 'Hello, Elise. I'm sorry, sir,' she apologised to Chris, 'I didn't mean to be rude asking you to wait outside.'

'I perfectly understand,' he insisted.

'It's just that, well, after all the trouble, I really don't want to do anything wrong.'

Joan had reinstated Maureen on the understanding that there was no repetition of her previous activities and now Maureen was anxious to make amends for all that had occurred.

'Joan will be joining us upstairs, Maureen. I've sent Angelique to find her,' Elise explained. 'Can you close up the shop for her? If there are any problems you know where we are.'

She caught a glimpse of Gary lurking

in the storeroom.

'I hope you don't mind,' Maureen said quietly, 'only, Joan's been doing paperwork most of the day and, well, Gary is keen to wipe the slate clean, like me. I don't know what got into us really. I suppose it was a moment's madness. Harry's that pleased the cricket club aren't taking the matter further as well.'

'This is Chris Saunders,' Elise introduced them. 'He's part of the public relations team for the developers.'

'Pleased to meet you.' Chris shook her hand. 'Really you have no need to worry on our behalf,' he said. 'We don't intend interfering with the farm shop or the cricket club in any way. We only want to benefit the community.'

Leaving a much-relieved looking Maureen to attend to her work, Elise and Chris went upstairs. Kyle, Angie and Joan soon followed them. Within moments Elise was whipping up one of her fish specials and Chris was laying out his plans on the table. Angie and

Kyle poured over them while Joan and Elise attended to the cooking.

'You can see the holiday caravans and cabins will be part of an exclusive venture,' Chris explained. 'We intend making them available only to accredited nature lovers. Merritt's Wood will be a perfect location for them. Rangers will regularly patrol the area and we don't foresee any trouble or interference with the day-to-day activities of Beech Mead. As I've already said the village will benefit, as the holidaymakers will bring in much needed business for the area. We intend introducing a youth scheme as well. We want to involve students — people like you, Kyle and Angie — in all our projects.'

'It looks a good plan,' Kyle said. 'What do you think, Angie?'

'Me too,' Angie replied. 'I wouldn't want one of the big companies to start building houses on the site.'

'That's not part of our plan at all,' Chris insisted. 'Conservation is our main issue.'

Although her 'date' with Chris turned out to be very different from how she imagined it would be, Elise was glad he included Kyle and Angie in his ideas. He seemed to have a natural affinity with the youngsters and listened to their thoughts and hopes for the area.

'I'm looking forward to moving here,' he said as he demolished the last of Elise's fish stew. 'It seems a really friendly place and it'll be nice to have a base rather than living out of a suitcase.'

'Do you live alone?' Joan asked.

'My wife has been staying with her mother while we've been house hunting. My mother-in-law has been a great help looking after the baby. She's six months old. Would you like to see a picture of her? Her name's Molly.'

Elise half expected Angie to groan and was ready to flash a warning at her daughter, but it wasn't necessary. Soon everyone was cooing over the pictures.

'Is this your wife?' Elise asked.

'Yes, that's Clare. She's hoping to come down for the summer fair at Hay Hall and then we'll spend the rest of the week house hunting.'

'Good,' Joan nodded. 'We'll all look forward to meeting her.'

'I'd be more than pleased to show her around if you're busy,' Elise offered.

'Thank you, that would be lovely. I've applied for a week off but in this business plans get changed at a moment's notice.'

'I'd best be going,' Kyle shuffled to his feet. 'Dad said I wasn't to be late.'

'I'll give you a lift if you like,' Chris offered. 'It's time I took my leave as well. Thank you for the meal, Elise and Joan, it was good to meet you.'

★ ★ ★

'What a pleasant young man,' Joan said as Angie saw them off downstairs. 'I expect you're glad to learn that he's got a family — or did you know about them already?'

144

'I've only met him once,' Elise said. 'I didn't know anything about his personal circumstances.'

'Did I see Mark driving off in a hurry?' Joan asked as she wiped up a plate.

'He had to go back to the station,' Elise replied. 'We thought we spotted Jacques Dubois in the crowds at the fair. Mark wanted to check through one or two things at work.'

'Really? So he'll be in touch again later I presume? You can tell him Chris is married so there's no need for him to drive off like that again, can't you?'

Elise rarely snapped at Joan but she was on the verge of delivering a sharp put down about the situation between herself and Mark being none of her business, when Seth poked his head around the door.

'Angie said I'd find you here,' he said. 'Mind if I come in?'

'There's some fish stew left if you'd like it,' Elise offered, grateful for the interruption.

'Lovely,' Seth beamed at her. 'I thought retirement would be a leisurely time but it's been meetings all day,' he said as he ladelled out the stew. 'I thought you'd like to be the first to know that the cricket club has decided to sell off part of its land. The money will come in useful for new equipment and the clubhouse is sorely in need of repair. It was a majority vote.'

'Oh, what a pity — you've just missed Chris Saunders,' Joan said. 'The public relations man — remember, he was the speaker at the meeting? He's been showing us their plans and they look very good. I think the club has made the right decision.'

'I hope things will begin to settle down now,' Seth said as he began to attack his plate of stew. 'This is good,' he complimented Elise. 'One thing I'll say for the French, they certainly know how to cook. My late wife, bless her heart, wasn't a natural in the kitchen.'

'I've been thinking, Seth,' Joan said slowly as she joined him at the table. 'If and when this holiday home thing takes off, I presume . . . well, that there'll be money in it?'

'Yes, of course. You own the land don't you? They have to make us all a reasonable offer.'

'In that case, I'd like to use the proceeds of the sale to set up a new drop-in leisure centre.'

'In Beech Mead?' Elise asked.

'Yes. I've seen the way the youngsters hang around with nothing to do. Not all of them are as level-headed as Angie and Kyle and I wouldn't want them to get into trouble. You know the sort of temptations that are around these days?'

'I think that's a wonderful idea,' Elise enthused.

'Yes, but it would mean a lot of work,' Seth warned Joan.

'I don't mind that. I've always worked hard and after this business with Maureen, I feel she might like to take on a bit more responsibility in the shop. That would free up some of my time to be a sort of consultant. I wouldn't do anything without your approval of course, Seth, but what do you think of it?'

'I'm with Elise on this one,' Seth agreed. 'Out of season when I'm not so tied up with the cricket club I have plenty of time on my hands too and I think a community project will really benefit the area.'

'That's settled then. Now, we really must go and leave Elise and Angie to get on with their evening.'

Elise stifled a yawn. 'It has been a busy day,' she agreed. After her early start and the fresh air of the fair and the ensuing drama, all she craved was a warm bath and an early night.

'You go ahead, Mum,' Angie called through from her bedroom. 'I'm doing some course work.'

Relieved that her daughter was at last getting down to her studies, Elise sat on her bed and brushed her luxuriant chestnut brown hair. Peter had always liked to run his hands through it. 'It's such a beautiful colour,' he would murmur.

These days Elise was forced to concede that the maintenance of the colour required the expertise of her hairdresser, but she liked to keep it long and well conditioned, but living close to the sea, frequent visits to the salon were a necessity, not a luxury. After only a day by the sea, she could feel the salt had started to dry out her hair and she searched for her intensive treatment shampoo.

Peter's picture smiled down at her from its place on her bedside cabinet. She remembered so clearly the day the photograph had been taken. They had gone for a day trip to Antibes, the sea had been a dazzling blue and they'd wandered along the seafront admiring the expensive yachts in the harbour.

'One day perhaps we'll own one of those.' Peter had pointed to an impressive pleasure craft.

'I think I'd rather have a small rowing boat on a little lake,' Elise replied.

'Perhaps you're right,' Peter agreed and took her hand. 'Race you to the tower — last one there buys the ice cream!'

She had taken the photo of Peter in the old town, the gentle breeze rifling his hair as he laughed back at her attempts to get him to pose properly.

Elise smiled at the memory. Angie had almost been too young to remember her father and her daughter had no issues with Elise's relationship with Mark. Was it time to move on?

When Mark had proposed to her she had not been ready and her answer had been an impulsive reaction, but ever since she had known Mark he had shown himself to be kind and considerate. Was she ready now to return his feelings?

But did he still love her? Was that the reason he had raced out of the car park after he had learned of her 'date' with Chris? Surely he wasn't jealous? They had agreed to be open in their relationship — so why did the thought of him with another woman cause Elise concern? Was this what it was like to fall in love the second time around?

Joan had found happiness with Seth after having been married to Richard for many years. Did she have qualms? It was too personal an issue to discuss with her, but Elise sensed that, when Seth and Joan married, all their lives would change.

'Where are you?' Angie called down the corridor.

'In my bedroom.'

'Haven't you had your bath yet?'

'Sorry,' Elise apologised, 'I was sorting through some things and I lost track of time.'

'Chris seems nice,' Angie said. 'Fancy him being married.'

'I'll look forward to meeting his family,' Elise replied.

'So you and Mark . . . ' Angie hinted.

Elise looked up at her daughter. 'What about us?'

'Are you still an item? I mean you get

151

on so well together and I don't mind, really.'

'What about Kyle?' Elise asked carefully.

'He would be happy too. His mother is getting married again and I think he'd like to see Mark fixed up too.'

'Fixed up?' Elise queried.

'Oh, you know what I mean. Anyway I thought I ought to tell you that Kyle was going to introduce Chris to Mark if he was back at the flat.'

'And has he?'

'Yes, he texted me. Has Mark contacted you?'

'No,' Elise replied in a hollow voice. 'There's been nothing.'

'That's men for you,' Angie smiled. 'I expect he's got his mind on other things. Well, if you're not going to take advantage of a hot bath, I am.'

Elise pressed the message button on her mobile phone. The inbox was empty. It had been two hours since Chris had driven Kyle home and it looked as though Mark hadn't found a free moment to contact her.

In the bath she could hear Angie singing along to the latest hit of her favourite girl band. Going into the hall she checked the answer phone in the vain hope that she had failed to hear the telephone ring. There was nothing.

It was all the confirmation she needed that Mark had taken her refusal to marry him as final and that they could have no future together.

Elise hadn't realised quite how much it would hurt.

10

The poised young woman greeted Elise with a confident, 'Hello — I'm Rosamund Strong. Are you Joan Trent?'

'No,' Elise replied, trying not to look too surprised. Rosamund did not resemble the usual farm shop visitor. She looked more like a lady who lunched, extremely together. With her eye for fashion detail Elise could tell her clothes were purchased from the more expensive end of the market and she was displaying a discreet designer logo on her handbag.

'Can I help? I'm her daughter-in-law. I'm standing in for her.'

'I see. Well I'm really here to introduce myself. My sister, Mrs Wainwright and her husband Commander Wainwright, Charles and Daphne, are the new purchasers of Hay Hall.'

Rumours had been flying round

Beech Mead for days now. The latest buzz was that the house had been sold and several of the more active gossipmongers suspected it would be converted into flats. Elise was relieved to learn this would not be so. She had feared her daughter might be looking for a new cause now the fuss over Merritt's Wood had died down.

'Elise Trent.' She held out a hand. 'Tell me, do you intend living at the Hall with your sister and her husband?'

'Only until they're settled in. There's such a lot to do since the place was in a dreadful state of repair. Charles is rather keen on DIY which is useful and he's looking to keep his days occupied now he's retired.'

'The last owners were elderly and when they moved out their family didn't put much in the way of resources into it.'

'You can say that again. Actually, another reason for my visit was to tell Mrs Trent that my sister and her husband do still intend to host the annual summer fair. Obviously we can't use the house; it's not really convenient and we're not sure how structurally sound certain parts of it are, but we do intend to put up a marquee on the lawn.'

'That's good news,' Elise enthused. 'The summer fair has been a tradition for as long as anyone can remember.'

'My sister also thought it would be a good opportunity to introduce the family to the community. As I understand it Mrs Trent usually judges the vegetable competition?'

'She has done for several years now.'

'Then I hope that will be another tradition we can maintain?' Rosamund smiled. 'Pardon me, but you're French, aren't you?'

'It's my accent isn't it?' Elise said with a smile. 'I've lived in England for years, but I've never been able to lose it.'

'I think it's very attractive and I love France. I always go skiing every winter if I can.'

'Are you married?' Elise asked.

'Heavens no. No time. I'm strictly a bachelor girl,' Rosamund flashed her dark brown eyes at Elise. 'I like to play the field.' She glanced at her watch. 'I must fly. I'm sorry to have missed Mrs Trent — Joan, I mean. Here's my sister's card. Perhaps you'd like to come up for drinks one Sunday to talk things through?'

'You want me there as well?'

'Of course — the more the merrier! We really want to integrate into the community.'

'Thank you, Ms Strong.'

'Rosamund, please — and may I call you Elise?'

'Of course.'

'Good. Now I must go.' She paused in the doorway. 'By the way you don't happen to know any security consultants do you?'

'I'm sorry, I don't,' Elise replied.

'No matter. It's just that my brother-in-law has some rather valuable artefacts and there's no efficient alarm system installed at the Hall. A friend of his recently lost some antique clocks after a break-in and Charles thought his first priority should be to get the house adequately protected.'

'Well, there is Mark Hampson.'

'Who's he?'

'One of our local policemen.'

'Do you have his number?' Elise scrawled it on a paper bag and passed it over. 'Thanks. I'll give him a bell. Bye.'

Her perfume lingered on the air after she'd gone. Elise wrinkled her nose; it was not one of her favourites. She remembered it from her days working as a student in an up-market boutique when her duties included tidying the make-up counter. The aroma was too heavy for her taste and always gave her a headache. Elise smiled. These days, if she were perfectly honest, she preferred the smell of the home grown organic vegetable display.

'I must be turning into a country bumpkin,' she murmured to herself, wondering how much longer Joan's appointment would be. With Maureen away on holiday, Joan was temporarily in sole charge and Elise had offered to step in even though she had a backlog of paperwork to catch up on.

She debated phoning Mark and mentioning Rosamund to him. After their day out at the fairground, they had only spoken on the phone once or twice. Mark had briefly informed her that the antiques ring was taking up a lot of his time and he wouldn't be around quite so much. Kyle, too, was not seeing quite so much of Angie now the heat behind the protest had died down. Elise wondered if both father and son were distancing themselves from the Trents.

A community bus pulled into the car park and Elise realised with a sinking heart it was Tuesday, the day Joan offered a discount to the senior citizens. Maths had never been one of Elise's strengths and she'd found the older generation liked a bargain when it came to their fruit and vegetables. Totting up their purchases was a challenge she was not looking forward to.

'Hello there,' the first of the new arrivals greeted her. 'Joan not here today?'

'She should be back later,' Elise informed the driver.

'Did she mention we're booked in for a light lunch?'

Elise's spirits perked up. Lunch was the one thing she was good at. 'Of course. Come this way.'

* * *

'Sorry, dear,' Joan's voice sounded breathless as Elise picked up the telephone. 'There's so much detail in the paperwork you wouldn't believe it. I meant to get back this afternoon, but we've only just finished.'

'That's all right,' Elise replied genuinely.

'Were you terribly busy?' Joan persisted, concerned.

'You could say that. Thirty lunches

and fifteen cream teas, not to mention a run on your new potatoes.'

'Heavens!' Joan squawked down the line. 'The Daffodils.'

'Exactly.' Elise leaned back and rubbed her aching feet. 'One little detail you forgot to mention.'

'I'll make it up to you I promise.'

'No problem,' Elise smiled. 'I actually enjoyed it, but they've only just gone a few minutes ago.'

'It's half past six,' Joan protested.

'I know but I couldn't lock up while we still had customers.'

'You've done a good day's business.' Joan sounded pleased. 'Seth sends you his love, by the way and said to tell you our plans for the community centre are taking shape, but he was right, it's going to be a lot of work.'

'When will you be back?' Elise asked. 'I haven't cashed up.'

'Leave all that to me. You take the evening off. Actually, if you don't mind, I won't be back tonight . . . '

'Not coming home?' Elise teased.

'What sort of talk is that, then? If you were Angelique I'd be delivering a lecture.'

'We had some wine at lunchtime and Seth wants to go out to dinner to celebrate our new deal, so he really doesn't feel like driving back and I haven't got transport because ... oh dear, it sounds like I'm making excuses, doesn't it?'

'Joan, I'm a French woman and we understand how to enjoy ourselves. You don't have to explain your motives. I'll open up in the morning if you're not back, but I do have to go into college later tomorrow morning.'

'I'll be back bright and early. Seth's got a cricket club meeting so there's no problem there.'

'By the way, we had a visitor ... Rosamund Strong.'

'Not another appointment I forgot about?'

'Her sister and brother-in-law are the new owners of Hay Hall,' Elise reminded her.

'You'll have to tell me all about it later, dear,' Joan said. 'Seth's ready to leave.'

'Hi, Mum.' Angie strolled into the kitchen. 'Is that Nan playing dirty old stop out?'

'Angelique!' Elise reprimanded her daughter. 'I won't have you talking about your grandmother like that.'

'Why should she get away with it,' Angie pouted, 'when I have to be in by ten o'clock?'

'Just because,' Elise laughed and nudged her mug towards her daughter. 'If you're making the tea, I'll have another cup. I'm exhausted. Those Daffodils ladies certainly know how to eat and drink. I'm afraid they demolished all my freezer stocks so it's going to be omelettes all round tonight.'

'I don't know what the older generation is coming to,' Angie tutted, 'but as you're keeping me on starvation rations would it be all right if I snaffled some of the leftover cakes from the fresh bakery in the shop?'

'If you can find any,' Elise retaliated. 'I'll have an éclair.'

'Mum . . . ' Angie tutted.

'I didn't get any lunch,' Elise defended herself.

With the remains of their scratch supper littering the table Elise and Angie caught up on the day's events.

'So, we have a glamorous female residing at Hay Hall,' Angie finished the last cake.

'I met her today. She came into the shop.'

'Is she the one Kyle was talking about?' Angie asked.

'Kyle's met her too?'

'There was a message in his voice mail. He picked up Mark's telephone by mistake this morning. Mark wasn't too pleased about it actually,' Angie grinned.

A loud knock at the door made them both jump.

'Are you expecting anyone?' Elise asked.

'Actually I am . . . I forgot to tell

you.' She slid a mobile phone across the table towards her mother. 'Mark said he'd be calling round to pick up his mobile. It's a long story so I'll get the door, shall I? Honestly, it comes to something when my mother and grandmother both have dates for the evening and I get stuck with boring old exam revision.'

'I do not have a date.' Elise began wishing her daughter had given her a little more notice and hoped her hair did not resemble a bird's nest.

'Can't hear you,' Angie trilled down the corridor. 'Hi, Mark. Come on in. Mum's expecting you so I'll make myself scarce.'

'Sorry,' Elise apologised attempting to tidy up the kitchen table. 'Despite what my daughter said, I didn't know you were due to visit until literally a moment ago.'

Mark looked tired as he sat down at the table. 'Kyle told me you had my phone.'

'I didn't actually, but I do now since

Angelique has just given it to me. Would you like some bread and cheese?' Elise asked. 'I've a camembert and the remains of a crusty loaf. It's all I can offer you I'm afraid, but I'll see if I can find a tomato or two. It's been such a busy day in the shop.'

'A veritable banquet.' Mark smiled as he watched Elise bustle around the worktop. 'Sorry I haven't been in touch but this Jacques Dubois business is hotting up. We've several new leads and you were right — it was him you saw at the fairground.'

'How do you know?'

'We had a tip off. Sorry, can't reveal our sources.'

Mark's mobile rang from where he'd left it on the table. 'Hello?' he made a thank you gesture to Elise as she put down the plate of bread and cheese. 'Yes. Sorry. I've been lost without my telephone all day. Miss Strong isn't it?' Elise stiffened, then, not wanting to overhear what he was saying, turned on the taps to drown out his voice.

Mark was still talking by the time Elise had dried the last plate. 'I'll look forward to our date,' she heard Mark say before he finished the call.

He cut himself some cheese and chewed thoughtfully before speaking again. 'I understand you put Miss Strong onto me?'

'She came into the shop this morning. Joan wasn't here, so I spoke to her.'

'We're having dinner tomorrow night at The Boathouse.' Elise raised her eyebrows. 'That's what I thought,' Mark agreed with a wry smile. 'Expensive — and it's her treat.'

'She's an expensive lady I'd say.'

'Do you think I'm in with a chance?' Mark speared another piece of cheese with his knife. 'What's the opposite of a sugar daddy? A toy boy, I suppose . . . though I reckon I'm a bit old to be one of those.'

Although he was joking, the thought of Mark and Rosamund together on a date was disturbing.

'I think she wants to discuss her brother-in-law's security arrangements with you.'

'She made no mention of it,' Mark sighed, 'but you're probably right. Rich and beautiful women wouldn't be interested in the likes of me.'

Elise bit down a retort. Even though lines of tiredness etched the corners of his eyes and he badly needed a shave, in her opinion his masculinity would have attracted any female. Elise now knew she was in love with Mark, but he would no longer be interested in her. She had turned down his proposal and given him to understand in no uncertain terms that she was not ready for re-marriage. Since then they had enjoyed a companionable existence, mainly through their children, but now Rosamund Strong was on the scene, Elise suspected Mark would have far less spare time for her.

Elise took a deep breath and said, 'We should have dinner together some time.' She wasn't used to making a date with a man and was uncertain if her suggestion would be welcome. But Mark was pre-occupied as he inspected his phone messages. 'Did you hear what I said?' Elise persisted.

'Right. Yes. Of course.' Mark looked up, smiling distractedly. 'I've got rather a lot of messages to catch up on. I hope you won't mind if I take my leave now.' He held up his telephone. 'I've got what I came for and I'm sure you've got a busy evening ahead of you.'

'Yes, of course.' Elise accepted it for the diplomatic turn down that it was.

'Thank you for the cheese supper. Quite the nicest meal I've ever tasted. Don't worry, I'll see myself out.'

Too proud to follow him down the corridor Elise remained where she was. As she heard the door to the flat close she realised any hopes she had regarding a renewal of her relationship with Mark had been well and truly dashed.

11

Hay Hall was rather a grand name for the turn of the twentieth century family property bordering the forest. It sat in mature gardens, boasting a lake, summerhouse and an arbour. Elise always enjoyed driving past it but no way was it a baronial hall.

Those in the know said the original owner had delusions of grandeur, an entrepreneur who hoped to earn himself a knighthood by doing good works. Whether or not he ever attained that honour, no one seemed too sure. The name Hay Hall had lived on long after the original owner's name had disappeared into the annals of history.

The new owners, Charles and Daphne Wainwright, were a couple in their late fifties with a large extended family, both having come to the marriage from previous partners. As far as Elise could make out, a constant stream of visitors invaded their house every weekend. She had never been able to ascertain who exactly was related to whom. A different member of the family answered the front doorbell every time she called. They were all as charming as each other and made her feel welcome.

'I only called,' Elise began as a stunning teenage girl smiled at her, 'to say that Joan Trent, my mother-in-law, would be delighted to judge the vegetable competition and to ask if there's there anything you need her to do beforehand?'

'Cool,' the girl answered, adding, 'I shouldn't think so. Gramps has got the marquee sussed and Granty — that's what I call Daphne. She's a sort of honorary Granny cum Aunty. Gramps is my real grandad but it gets seriously complicated after that — even I can't work it out.' She giggled then carried on with her rambling chat. 'Anyway, Granty has got lists and stuff all over the place. Do you want to have a word with her? Or scary Aunt Rosamund? I'm really glad she's not a proper aunt. I borrowed one of her tops once and she went, like, ballistic . . . said it was designer or something.' The girl ground to a halt and shrugged. 'Sorry . . . what was the question again?'

'Oh, don't worry. I'll call again.' Elise smiled warmly. 'I know everyone must be very busy, so I won't hold them up.'

'Just as well.' A dimple deepened in the girl's cheek. 'I'm not sure where anyone is . . . Hi Kyle!' She waved at a new arrival.

Elise spun round at the sound of feet on the gravel behind.

'Hi, Cherry, Elise.' He grinned at her.

'What are you doing here?' Elise asked.

'I've come to take Cherry out. You know, show her the sights of Beech Mead.'

'Shouldn't take too long,' Cherry giggled again. 'It's like sticksville here.'

'I didn't know you two knew each

other,' Elise said.

'We met when Kyle's father came round to discuss security with Rosamund,' Cherry said airily. 'Hang on, Kyle — be with you in two ticks.'

'So, how're things?' Kyle asked Elise while he waited.

'Hopefully settled down for the moment.'

Kyle cleared his throat. 'I think you ought to know . . . Dad and Rosamund . . . well . . . ' He shuffled his feet. 'They didn't only discuss security stuff . . . you know?'

'It's all right, Kyle, I understand.'

'Course you do.' A look of relief swept across Kyle's face. 'I keep forgetting you're French . . . they know about these things.' He turned as Cherry reappeared in the doorway. 'Ready?'

Cherry's only concession to going out appeared to be to sport a deep red beret. Elise liked her sense of style.

'Give my love to Angie,' Kyle called as Cherry closed the front door behind them.

'Oh — you're Angie's mother?' Cherry's baby blue eyes widened. 'I should have known. She was singing your praises at the open session.'

'What open session was this and why was I not invited?'

'Have I put my foot in it?' Cherry turned a pretty rosy shade of pink. 'Sorry.'

'You were probably working, Elise,' Kyle said in an attempt to defuse the situation.

''Cos we're new to the area we got an invite.' Cherry began talking again. 'I went along as Granty's guest. Angie's stuff is brilliant. She said she inherited her fashion sense from her French mother — I had no idea that was you. She really wants to go on to fashion college and her teacher says she's the best pupil in her class.'

'Come on, Cherry,' Kyle tugged at her elbow. 'See you around, Elise.'

Elise made her way back to her car, her head full of all that the two young people had told her. According to Kyle,

174

Mark and Rosamund were seeing a lot of each other — that would explain why her mobile had been so quiet — and Kyle appeared to be involved with Cherry.

In a way she was pleased about that; her daughter was far too young to go steady romantically with anyone — and from what Cherry had intimated Angie now seemed to be concentrating on her studies again.

She turned her car towards the language school, determined to spend the rest of the day devoted to her long outstanding 'to do' list. Ever since her stint in the shop covering for Maureen, Elise had been fighting a losing battle to get on top of it.

She tapped her fingers on the steering wheel. She absolutely would not think about Mark and Rosamund Strong; there was far too much else going on in her life. Now Angie had reapplied herself to her course work Elise needed to be on hand to help in any way she could. Joan too was always looking for assistance in the shop and then there was her work. She had plenty to occupy her time and plenty to take her mind off Mark Hampson.

★　★　★

The day of the summer fair dawned with all the promise of beautiful weather. Everyone had been holding their breath all week in the hope that the sunny spell wouldn't break.

'We don't want a typical English summer do we?' Joan looked out the window, as she and Elise were getting ready.

'Don't we?' Elise said.

'Three hot days and a thunder storm,' Joan smiled at her.

Elise shuddered. She hated thunderstorms. In her part of the world they could at times be extremely violent and she still remembered as a child how frightened she would get when lightning split the sky and thunder rumbled round the mountains for hours before the rain poured down.

'Is Angie making her own way there?' Joan asked.

'Yes. She and her classmates are presenting some sort of revue during the tea break interval, so it's final dress rehearsal.'

'That should be fun.' Joan did a final check on her equipment. 'It always pays to take your own clipboard, pens and papers on these occasions,' she said. 'I do hope I don't upset anybody with my judging. Some people can get most unpleasant if they don't win. I've been accused of all sorts of things.'

'Like being bribed with an aubergine?' Elise laughed.

'You'd be surprised,' Joan said with a dark look.

A sharp ring on the shop bell interrupted them. 'Who can that be?' Joan mused. 'Everyone knows we're closed for the day.'

'It's Chris Saunders,' Elise said looking out of the window.

'I've come to offer you a lift to the

Hall,' he called up. 'Clare and Molly are already there.'

'We'll be right down,' Elise called back.

'I don't actually need a lift,' Joan said. 'Seth is calling for me in five minutes. Besides, if I try to get into that car you'll need a tin opener to get me out.' She nodded to Chris's convertible.

'If you're sure?' Elise hesitated.

'You go with Chris, Elise. Seth can bring us all home if you need a lift back.'

'All set?' Chris asked once Elise had wriggled into the passenger seat.

'It's like sitting in a bucket. I'm surprised Clare lets you drive a car like this now you have a daughter,' Elise said, straightening her skirt that had ridden up during the manoeuvre.

'My one legacy of my bachelor days,' Chris admitted with a laugh. 'But you're right. It's going to have to go. It's hopelessly impractical now I'm a father. So one last burn up in the old girl?'

He pressed the accelerator and they

shot forward into the road. Elise was glad she was wearing a scarf as the top of the convertible was down and the wind would have played havoc with her hair.

But the feel of the warm air on her face made her smile and for a moment she was transported back to the days of her youth when, before she had met Peter, various boyfriends would race her round the circuitous mountain roads at eye-watering speeds in an effort to impress her with their prowess.

Chris was a fast but skilful driver and Elise enjoyed the journey. They slowed up as they reached the outskirts of Hay Hall — the road was clogged with pedestrians, as well as vehicles of every description.

'Is it always this manic?' Chris asked as he was forced to swerve out of the path of an excited child who wasn't looking where she was going. The mother gave an apologetic shrug as she grabbed the toddler by the hand. Chris acknowledged the apology and joined the queue, inching slowly forward.

'I suppose everyone wants to see the new owners,' Elise said. 'I've heard Daphne's pulled out all the stops. There's going to be a Punch and Judy show for the children, a fortune telling tent and my daughter, Angelique, is doing a revue.'

'Sounds a gas.' Chris laughed. 'Is that someone waving at you by the gate?'

Elise shaded her eyes against the sun. 'It's Rosamund. She's Daphne Wainwright's sister.'

'Isn't that your policeman friend with her? Kyle introduced us when I gave him a lift home. It looks like she's got him on car parking duties.' Chris hooted in response to Rosamund's wave as he slowed down.

'Back again,' she raised an eyebrow at him, 'with another woman in tow? What's your secret?'

'My charm, what else?' Chris bantered back at her.

'Mark, darling,' Rosamund called

over, 'can you show Chris where to park?'

Elise was left with the uncharitable suspicion that Mark had parked them as far as possible from the scene of the action and so close to a tree it was almost impossible for her to climb out.

'Come on,' Chris urged Elise, not seeming to notice the slight. 'I'll introduce you to Clare and Molly. Then I'm going to have to leave you for a while. Duty calls I'm afraid. So many people want a piece of me now the development is going through. You've no idea what a popular chap I am!'

Chris took her hand as she picked their way through a muddy section of grass. Elise bit her lip; what was the matter with Mark, parking them in what almost amounted to a pigsty?

'Surely Mark could have parked us nearer the house?' Elise hopped around on one foot as she inadvertently stepped out of her sandal. 'Pah, I hate mud!'

'Steady there.' Chris put his arms

round her to steady her just as Mark looked across.

'Thank you so much,' Elise beamed up at Chris and gave him the full benefit of her smile. She clung onto Chris's arm for a few seconds longer than was necessary. If Rosamund Strong was going to call Mark 'darling', then two could play at that game! Not that Elise had any intention of flirting with Chris, she thought. He was a happily married man — but she wasn't sure if Mark knew that.

'I believe there are some corporate parking spaces on the forecourt,' Chris admitted, 'but I like to get down and dirty with the ordinary people.'

'We're certainly dirty,' Elise admitted with a laugh as she looked down at her mud bespattered sandals, 'still it's nothing a little water won't wash away.'

'Ready for the off now?' Chris asked once she'd refastened her sandal.

'Ready,' Elise replied. She looked to where Mark had been standing but there was no sign of him.

* * *

Clare Saunders was a pleasant if shy woman standing on her own by the marquee pushing a baby buggy.

'Sorry, darling,' he put a proprietary arm around her waist. 'This is Elise and she got stuck in the mud.'

'I've had better introductions,' Elise laughed, immediately taking to Chris's wife. 'It's my fault we're late. I do apologise.'

'I know where there's a stand pipe,' Clare said. 'Molly got in a bit of a mess with a choc ice. It's over here.'

'Can I leave you girls to it?' Chris asked. 'I promise to be back later. Bye, darling.' He kissed Molly's broderie anglaise sunhat and stroked his wife's arm.

'This is very kind of you,' Clare smiled at Elise as they made their way to the fresh water tap. 'I'm not very good at making the first move and although everyone looks friendly I haven't spoken to a soul yet.'

'Would Molly like to see the Punch and Judy show?' Elise asked, smiling down at the toddler. 'There'll be lots of other mums there, I'm sure.'

'Sounds like a good place to start,' Clare said.

Soon a circle of other mothers pushing buggies and chatting together welcomed Clare and Molly into their midst. Elise, glad to see that Clare seemed to be enjoying herself and that Molly had already made some new friends, made her excuses, promising to return later.

'What a crush.' Rosamund appeared from behind a tea tent. She was wearing a floral creation that floated with the curves of her body. Elise had chosen a plain blue dress and felt rather dowdy compared to the peacock colours of Rosamund's outfit. 'I had quite forgotten how country people so enjoy this sort of bean feast.'

'Have you finished parking?'

'I've left Mark to it. It was too much like hard work. Besides, I'm needed in the house. Cherry is being a bit difficult, something to do with one of the children spilling orange juice down her new outfit. Daphne asked if I'd go and soothe the trouble waters. I don't know how she does it — Daphne I mean. I might have to have a lie down afterwards. I find teenagers very wearing, don't you?'

'I have a teenage daughter . . . ' Elise began, but Rosamund wasn't listening.

'By the way,' she asked breezily, 'there's nothing between you and Mark is there?'

'We work together occasionally,' Elise said, deliberately misunderstanding the question.

'I meant of a personal nature. I would hate to upset the applecart if there is, only . . . ' she all but purred, 'we've grown quite close. He's been immensely helpful over our security arrangements and we've spent several evenings together discussing options. He's a very attractive man, isn't he? I'd like to move the relationship forward, if you get my drift.'

'There's nothing of a romantic nature between Mark and myself,' Elise assured her, wishing it didn't hurt so much to admit the truth. The expression on Rosamund's face reminded Elise of the cat that got the cream.

'Good. That's all right then,' she said, then swept an arm in the direction of the festivities. 'Do enjoy yourself. I've had just about enough bucolic entertainment for one afternoon.' And with that, she walked off, drifting towards the main house.

Tilting her chin defiantly, Elise found herself in the unusual position of caring about Mark's love life. She didn't want him getting involved with Rosamund. She had a nasty feeling it would all end in tears. If only she could warn him, as a friend, but he would never listen to her, not now after all that had passed between them.

Hearing laughter from the vegetable tent, Elise sauntered over to where the prize giving ceremony was about to begin.

Chris was hovering by the tent flaps. 'I've been told this is where the action is,' he greeted her. 'Great show, isn't it? Where are the girls?'

'I've left Clare and Molly watching the Punch and Judy show with several other young mums,' Elise explained.

'Good. I'll catch up with them when I can and we'll go for an ice cream. I spy two free seats. Come on.'

Grabbing Elise's hand before she had a chance to protest, she allowed Chris to lead her towards the recently vacated seats. Chris draped a casual arm around her shoulder as they settled down. His head touched hers as he whispered, 'Sorry to be so familiar, but there's not much room is there? I'm almost sitting in your lap.'

Politeness forced Elise to smile agreement but as she raised her eyes they clashed with Mark's who was sitting on the far side of Chris. 'Hello, Mark,' she acknowledged him. 'I thought you were in charge of the parking.' She smiled sweetly.

There was no answering smile in Mark's eyes. 'Obviously,' he replied before pointedly turning his back on the pair of them.

'Ssh,' Chris bumped his head against Elise's, 'the judging's about to start and we don't want to get chucked out for making a noise, although it would give us a good excuse to get a double choc chip ice cream, wouldn't it?'

The pair of them giggled like schoolchildren and it gave Elise a silly thrill of pleasure to see that, from the stiffening of Mark's shoulders, he had heard every word.

12

'And the winner for the best runner bean is number six,' Joan announced from the podium.

'Fixed!' a voice called out from the audience as Seth rose to collect his second prize of the afternoon.

'I can assure you all the judging is anonymous,' Joan insisted as she pinned the golden rosette onto Seth's lapel.

'That's what they all say,' someone from the cricket club joined in the banter as a ragged cheer greeted Seth's award.

'Do you think if I got engaged to Joan next summer I might win first in tomatoes?' one of the wicket keepers joked.

'You could always try,' another team member guffawed.

Elise clapped automatically, not really

registering what was happening on stage. Surely Mark didn't suspect there was anything between her and Chris? It was ridiculous.

Chris leaned in closer to make his voice heard above all the noise just as Mark chose that moment to turn around again. 'I really ought to go and find Clare and Molly. Will you be all right?'

'Of course,' Elise insisted, relieved that she wasn't going to have to spend the entire afternoon squashed up close to Chris.

After he'd squeezed past the chairs, Elise moved up to sit next to Mark. As he had again turned his back to her, she tapped him on the shoulder.

'Lost your companion?' he asked. There was no warmth or humour in his voice.

'For the moment, yes,' she replied. Mark blinked at her but didn't say anything in reply. 'Talking of companions . . . where's Rosamund?'

'At the moment I'm not sure.'

'I hear you're more than good friends these days . . . '

'Who told you that?' A slow smile stretched across Mark's face. 'You're scowling.'

'She did. And I am not scowling.'

'Yes you are, and if I didn't know you better, I would say you were actually jealous.'

The heat in the marquee began to make Elise feel uncomfortable. 'It's nothing to do with my feelings, it's just . . . ' a lump in her throat made it difficult for her to get the words out. 'Well, it's just that I suspect Rosamund is using you and I wouldn't like you to get hurt.'

'Thank you for your concern.' Mark was still smiling. 'There's no need for you to worry. I'm a big boy now and I can look after myself.' He stood up. 'Talking of Rosamund, now the judging is over, I'd better go and find her. She promised me a tour of the rose garden after the vegetable show was over.' He raised an eyebrow. 'Do you think she's going to propose?'

Aware that Mark was not taking her seriously, that he was actually laughing at her, Elise bit down a retort. 'Rosamund's not your type,' she hissed.

'And what gives you the right to decide that?' Mark asked. Sensing the tension between them, several people were beginning to glance in their direction. 'Now if you'll excuse me? I don't like to keep a lady waiting,' he added.

The touch of Mark's legs against her knees as she tried to move out of his way added to her discomfort. Elise didn't understand what was happening to her emotions. If she hadn't known better she would say she was jealous of Rosamund because she was in love with Mark and that was why she cared what happened to him. Was that so?

Things had been so different with Peter, but Mark and Peter were two very different men and neither was she the same young girl she had been when she had fallen for a penniless student.

She was a woman of almost forty now, who had been married and had a teenage daughter. Mark, too, was a father; they were both parents with responsibilities.

If this was love the second time around then it was very different from the first time.

She watched Mark make his way out of the tent. He didn't turn to look back at her and Elise realised she had no right to feel about him the way she did. He had asked her to marry him and she had turned him down. That was the end of the story and it was time she got a grip on her emotions.

Seeing Joan making her way towards her, Elise stood up.

'I'm glad that's over.' Joan fanned herself with a programme. 'I had no idea Seth had entered so many classes. I think next year we are going to have to limit his entries. Did you hear those comments from the cricket club members?'

'No one seriously suspected you of

anything underhand,' Elise assured her.

'Let's get some fresh air,' Joan suggested. 'These tents get so stuffy.'

'It's nearly time for Angelique's revue,' Elise looked at her watch. 'We mustn't miss that.'

'Where are they holding it?'

'She said if the weather was fine it would be by the lake.'

'What say we get a cup of tea first? I am absolutely parched, then we'll head towards the action.'

* * *

Benches had been ranged around the lake and taking advantage of the sunny afternoon the students had used the water as a natural backdrop for their production. It was obviously a welcome move as the benches were crammed with visitors all pleased to be enjoying the afternoon sunshine and looking forward to the revue.

Elise spied a be-hatted Mrs Newman and her husband Councillor Newman seated in the middle of the front row. She nudged Joan. 'She's wearing yet another unsuitable hat,' Elise whispered conspiratorially.

'Well don't upset her by telling her it looks like a flowerpot this time,' Joan said. 'And there's no need to look so innocent,' she added. 'Honestly you and Angie are a right pair. Mrs Newman and I are back on speaking terms and I'd like to keep things that way. Now,' Joan looked at her programme, 'what's this all about?'

'The revue is entitled A Day In The Life Of A Farm Shop,' Elise read out the title.

Joan raised her eyebrows. 'I do hope Angie doesn't make things too personal,' she whispered. 'I don't want any more trouble with the authorities.'

Elise felt a pang of concern, too. Angie had a wicked sense of humour that people didn't always understand.

But she needn't have worried. From the very first scene gales of laughter greeted the revue. The cricket club was parodied, as was the shop. There were several veiled references to local dignitaries, one of whom wound up in an undignified position in the vegetable garden after being chased by a chicken as he tried to retrieve a cricket ball. Elise stole a glance at the Newmans. She saw to her relief that they were joining in the laughter and, casting a sideways glance at Joan, the two women allowed themselves to relax.

Angie had gone to a lot of trouble and her efforts were well rewarded when the revue came to an end and the audience sprang to their feet to applaud her and her fellow actors.

'I think we have a major talent in the family,' Elise said.

'Peter was always good at play acting at school,' Joan said. 'I think he got his sense of theatre from his father. It looks like Angie has inherited it . . . Ah, here's Seth.'

'Things seem to be winding down,' he said. 'Shall we make tracks, if you're ready to leave?'

'I'd better go and find out what Angelique intends to get up to,' Elise said, 'and say goodbye to Chris.'

'Shall we meet by the gate in half an hour?' Seth suggested.

'What did you think of it, Mum?' Angie asked as Elise ran her to ground round the back of one of the garden sheds they had used as a changing room.

'I was very impressed.'

Angie went pink with pleasure. 'You're not just saying that?'

'Of course she isn't,' Cherry cut in. 'You're the business, Angie — look.' She jangled a charity bucket full of coins. 'I went round after the performance asking for spare cash and everybody put something in. They said we should have charged for putting on such a good show.'

'Your grandmother and Seth want to go home,' Elise said.

'Is it okay if I hang out with the guys for a while?'

'Gramps will drive us all back, Elise,'

Cherry offered. 'There's a lot of clearing up to do so he won't mind if we stay on to help him.'

'Very well. I'll see you later, then,' Elise agreed.

Making a private note to check that this was indeed the case, Elise trudged across the lawn to where groups of visitors were still gossiping. Cars were beginning to leave and there was a bit of a tail back in the car park.

'We had a lovely time,' Clare accosted Elise as she said goodbye to the Wainwrights and thanked them for their hospitality. Molly waved up at her, her face sticky with candy floss. 'I've got several email addresses and telephone numbers. Thank you so much for introducing me to everyone.'

'It was my pleasure. I know what it's like to come in from the outside. When I first moved here I was scared no one would understand my English, and now I couldn't imagine living anywhere else.'

Clare looked a little embarrassed and

lowered her voice. 'Chris certainly doesn't seem to have that problem . . . the ladies of the village kept plying him with tea and he was too polite to turn down their offers, you understand.'

'Tell him I said goodbye then, will you? And any time you feel like some company call by the farm shop. We'll show you around and I'm sure Molly will love the animals.'

'It's a date,' Clare promised.

Realising she was now late for Seth, Elise turned and hurried towards the gate.

'Got you!' a voice said as a pair of hands was clamped around her waist. As she turned, a kiss that was meant for her cheek — she hoped — was planted much closer to her lips than she would have liked.

'Chris?'

'Whoops, sorry! Accident!' He let go of her immediately. 'Thanks for all you've done for my girls. I'm very grateful. I'll be in touch.' He hurried away with no further explanation.

'There you are, Elise,' Seth called over from one of the tents. 'I've been looking for you everywhere. Where's Angie?'

'She's staying on with her friends to help clear up.'

★ ★ ★

'Would anyone like more tea?' Joan asked after they had all freshened up in her cottage.

'I would suggest something stronger but I'm driving,' Seth replied. 'Perhaps a soft drink?'

'You will stay won't you, Elise?' Joan pressed her. 'Seth and I need to discuss our forthcoming wedding arrangements and we'd like you to be in on them.'

'What exactly did you have in mind?' Elise asked.

'We thought perhaps a family affair in July? Seth's spoken to his son in Canada and he can fly over with his family. Then there's my sister and her family and various cousins . . . '

'What about the village? You'll have to invite them or they'll be mortally offended.'

'If we had the ceremony in the afternoon we could have an evening reception when we could invite everyone else. Do you think that would be a good idea?'

'I don't think the church hall would be big enough for our needs. There's a hotel the cricket club uses for its functions,' Seth explained. 'I'm sure they could fix us up but we'll have to do something soon because July can be a very busy time and it's only a month or so away.'

'Go for it,' Elise said. 'Angelique and I will be on hand to help with any arrangements and I'm sure we can rope in some of the students for any physical stuff.'

'I thought you'd say that,' Joan smiled. 'Another thing . . . you will help me with my outfit, won't you?' she asked with an anxious look on her face. 'I haven't a clue what to wear. All my outfits are strictly functional. When Richard was alive I had several dresses I could have worn, but now they look dated and half of them I can't get into and I don't want anything that highlights my bingo wings.'

'Your what?' Seth looked mystified.

'Don't worry about it, Seth. It's a female thing.'

'I'm sure you'll look lovely, whatever you wear,' Seth insisted.

'It can be my present to you,' Elise offered. 'And we must include Angelique — she has an excellent eye for detail.'

'Did I hear my name . . . ?'

'You're back early,' Elise looked round in surprise.

'We were discussing my wedding dress,' Joan explained. 'You will help, darling, won't you?'

'Just try leaving me out,' Angie said, helping herself to a handful of crisps.

'We'd better leave Seth and Joan to discuss the rest of their arrangements,' Elise got up.

'You haven't asked me why I'm back early,' Angie said swallowing her crisps.

'I presumed you'd finished clearing up,' Elise replied. 'Where's Commander Wainwright? Did he drive you back?'

'One of the tent guys gave me a lift.'

'Angelique,' Elise remonstrated with her, 'that was not our arrangement.'

'I know that, but I have mega news. Charles Wainwright couldn't give me a lift because he's been detained at Hay Hall. There's been another burglary.' Three pairs of eyes turned in Angie's direction. 'Up at the hall, this afternoon.'

'That's impossible.'

'No it isn't. With so much coming and going it would have been the easiest thing in the world for someone to nip unnoticed into the house. They could have pretended to be looking for the loo or delivering milk or something and no one would have been any the wiser. Everyone's attention was distracted by Gran's vegetable show, the Punch and Judy, then there was our revue, not to mention the fortune telling tent. Madame Zuleika was doing a roaring trade, so I hear.'

'What about the new alarm system that's just been fitted?' Elise demanded.

'It wasn't switched on because no one could remember the number and Mark said Daphne wasn't to write it down.'

'What's missing?' Seth asked.

'Charles's collection of clocks I think. It was all a bit chaotic so no one's too sure about anything. And what's more,' Angie added, 'Everyone who attended the fair today is a suspect!'

'But that means . . . ' Elise raised a hand to her face, ' . . . us.'

'Exactly,' Angie polished off what remained of the crisps. 'Now, did I hear you mention supper?'

13

Elise hesitated outside the neat semi-detached house. She had not been here before and was unsure of her reception. Mark's new house stood in a quiet side street of similar properties and, like the others, possessed a postage stamp front garden and off street parking, something she knew would appeal to Mark.

His flat had been very much a bachelor apartment, not suitable for sharing with his son, and the unconventional hours he worked also meant he needed constant access to his car, again something that could not be guaranteed if he had parked in the road outside. That was why, Elise supposed, when Mark's new home had come on the market he had moved so quickly and without telling her. She had only heard of his move through the Beech Mead grapevine.

Elise clutched her housewarming present of a potted chrysanthemum to her chest. At the time visiting Mark on the off chance seemed like a good idea, but now she wasn't so sure.

Would he be in? Would he even welcome a visit from her? There only one way to find out, she decided, before taking a deep breath and knocking loudly on the door. It was yanked open almost immediately.

'Elise!' Mark stepped back sharply in surprise. 'What are you doing here?'

'I won't come in if it's inconvenient.' Elise felt as gauche as a teenager on a first date as all the poise of her thirty-nine years deserted her in an instant.

'There's nothing wrong is there?'

'No, everything's fine. I, er . . . brought you this.' She thrust the plant at him. 'To welcome you to your new home.'

'Thank you,' he said. His fingertips grazed hers as he accepted the gift. Elise's fingertips tingled from the sensation of his touch. 'I'm sorry I haven't been in touch. What with one thing and another . . . ' he ran a hand through his hair making it spikier than usual. It had always been a joke between them that at last something about him was in fashion. 'I'm glad you found me.'

'Are you?' A smile trembled on Elise's lips.

'You don't know how much,' he replied in a soft voice.

The tightness in Elise's jaw eased and she realised she had actually been grinding her teeth, something she hadn't done since the days of her adolescence.

'Angelique told me about the robbery at Hay Hall,' she said after a short pause when she realised she couldn't carry on standing on his doorstep smiling without actually doing anything, 'and I wondered if I could be of any help.'

As ploys went it didn't have much going for it but Elise couldn't think of a better excuse to explain her reason for turning up out of the blue on his doorstep.

'How could you help?' Mark asked, frowning in puzzlement.

'I was there,' she finished lamely, 'and I . . . well . . . I know lots of other people were there but perhaps I saw something without realising it? I don't know . . .'

She noticed Mark's eyes were bloodshot and that he was repeatedly running a hand through his uncombed hair.

'Sorry,' he apologised for his appearance. 'I've only just come off duty. Come in. Why don't you make the coffee while I freshen up? I won't be long. Careful you don't fall over any of the tea chests. I haven't had time to unpack anything yet. What with all that's been happening I was lucky to be able to move at all.'

Elise navigated her way to the kitchen and after hunting down a jar of coffee and the kettle, sorted out two mugs and some milk. Mark joined her a few moments later, smelling of pine shower gel. His hair was wet and freshly shampooed and his eyes looked clearer.

'Exactly what I need,' he said scooping up one of the coffee mugs. 'Can I offer you a beach chair? They're a bit wobbly, so careful how you go.'

Elise perched on one chair and Mark eased himself back into the second.

'Are you allowed to say what happened at Hay Hall?'

'I expect you know almost as much as I do. With so many visitors it's very difficult to work out where everyone was. Lots of people had already left by the time the theft was discovered. It's an absolute nightmare.'

'I can imagine.'

'Actually there is something you can tell me.'

'Yes?'

'I don't suppose you heard anyone speaking in French?'

'No, I didn't.'

'It was only a long shot,' Mark said with a look of regret. 'There were reports of a car with French number plates parked around the back of the kitchen entrance. Kyle saw it too. He made a note of the number but like so much else in this case it's turned out to be false. It's nothing to do with the Wainwrights or any of their house guests so we suspected there might be a connection with the other robberies in the area.'

'I'm sorry, I can't help on that one.'

'What makes the whole thing so unfortunate was that I was there, all the time,' Mark said in exasperation, 'and I never noticed anything odd at all.'

'Your time was taken up with Rosamund,' Elise said, then felt rather cheap as she caught the flash of expression in Mark's blue eyes. 'I mean, you were parking cars and marshalling vehicles, weren't you?'

'If that comment was a veiled reference to my relationship with Rosamund,' Mark allowed himself a wry smile, 'then I have to tell you that it's history. Not that it was much to write home about in the beginning.'

'That's not how Rosamund was telling it.'

'Wasn't it?' Mark now seemed to be enjoying Elise's discomfort and she began to wish she hadn't been quite so outspoken about his relationship. 'Well for your information she asked me for my professional advice about installing a security system at Hay Hall. We went out to dinner two or three times, and apparently Rosamund had rather exceeded her authority in asking for my advice because Charles had already made his own arrangements — but I didn't realise this until after the break in.'

'Angie mentioned something about no one being able to remember the security code.'

'I feel I'm to blame on that one. I told Daphne that when her system was set up it would be wise not to write down the code where anyone could see it. She agreed with me. Unfortunately the downside was she followed my advice to the letter but that meant she also couldn't remember the code when it was her turn to switch on the system. If it wasn't such a serious situation, it would be funny.'

'You can't blame yourself, Mark. At the end of the day the Wainwrights are responsible for their own security.'

'That's the stance they're taking. They're being extremely reasonable about the whole thing, but it doesn't make me feel any better. I should have been able to do something.' Mark sighed. 'I really thought Kyle and I would be settled here — that's why I moved out of the flat so quickly.' He looked round the chaotic living room. 'Amanda's moving to Spain with her new husband and we thought it would be better for Kyle to stay with me permanently until he takes his exams at least. Now I'm not sure I'm going to be staying here.'

'Surely you're not thinking of moving again?' Elise said.

'I may have to. My superiors aren't

too happy with my performance on this one.'

'It wasn't your fault.' Elise could feel her temperature rising at the injustice of it.

'They don't see it like that. I was the man on the spot and I failed in my duty.'

'But you were off duty.'

'A policeman is never off duty.'

'That's outrageous!' Elise splashed some coffee on the table as she slammed down her mug. 'You have to do something about it. If we were in France there would be action. People would protest in the streets. It's not fair.'

'Where were you when I needed you to fight my cause?' Mark asked with a tired smile. 'Don't answer that,' he added. 'What you do in your spare time is none of my business ... how is Chris, by the way?'

'I don't know, I haven't seen him since the fair. He said he was going to be busy now the developers are moving in.'

'That's another thing. With things moving forward it's bringing lots of itinerant workers into the area creating a perfect cover for this antiques ring, since a new face doesn't cause any undue comment.'

A silence fell between them. Elise grew aware of a clock ticking in the background. She could hear children playing in the garden next door and the room smelt of tea chests. It was as if the tension between her and Mark heightened her senses. Her coffee was now cold and gritty and she grimaced as she swallowed some.

'Want me to get you some more?' Mark asked.

'No.' Elise shook her head. 'I should be going. I only called round to see how you were. Kyle told Angelique you were really busy. I wasn't sure you would be in and if you hadn't answered the door I was going to leave the plant on your porch.'

'Elise,' Mark began, 'I know it's none of my business, and I'm only sort of repaying the debt.'

'Sorry?'

'You warned me about Rosamund and I think it only fair to warn you in return.'

'About what?'

'You do know Chris Saunders is married?'

'I do,' Elise replied quietly, 'and the only reason I was with him at the fair was because he asked me to look after his wife and daughter. Clare's a bit shy and needed a nudge but once I introduced her to some other young mothers she was fine.'

'I see . . . '

'The day of the fair I left her watching the Punch and Judy show with her daughter. I bumped into Chris in the vegetable tent when I was looking for Joan. That's why we were together, and,' Elise added, 'I think it was really mean of you to park us in that pig sty place.'

A devilish smile softened Mark's tired face. 'I'm not proud of myself, there,' he admitted. 'It just got to me seeing the two of you together in his fancy car. You looked so beautiful with the wind in your hair and you were laughing with him and . . . well, sorry,' he repeated his apology.

'Why should it matter to you what I did with Chris?' Elise demanded. 'You were with Rosamund.'

'I've already explained that I wasn't.' Mark's reply was dangerously close to a snap, but then he sighed. 'Let's not go over old ground. You've made your feelings on re-marriage perfectly clear and I won't embarrass you again by telling you how I feel about you.'

His mobile phone interrupted them. While he took the call Elise cleared up the coffee mugs.

'I have to go. Work calls,' he said.

'On a Sunday? Didn't you say you'd only just come off duty?'

'I did but there have been some developments.'

'Would you . . . ?' Elise began, her plans for the day thwarted. She paused, wondering how to phrase the rest of her question.

Mark shrugged on his coat, began looking around for his keys and located them under a plant pot. 'Another housewarming present from the girls at work,' he said. 'It looks a bit wilted, doesn't it?'

'All it needs is some water. Here, give it to me.' Elise quickly doused it in tap water and picked off a few dead leaves.

'Thank you. I promise to look after your chrysanthemum with more care.' He put the plant back on the shelf. 'What were you about to say?' Mark paused by the front door.

'Dinner one night? You and me?' Elise asked in a rush before she lost her nerve. 'I did ask you the other day but I don't think you were listening.'

'Sorry,' he treated her to a devastating smile. 'I can think of nothing better than to have dinner with you — but I do have one important request.'

'Yes?'

'Can we make it a teenager free zone?'

Elise nodded. 'Kyle and Angelique can spend the evening with Joan.' She added with a slow smile, 'If they're stuck for something to do they can always help her pack up the organic vegetable boxes.'

'Excellent idea.' Mark strode towards his car. 'Give me a ring and we'll fix up a date.'

As he drove away Elise pondered yet again the strength of love the second time around. She had been so new to the emotion she hadn't recognised it for what it was, but now she realised it was the real thing.

Now how could she ever convince Mark of the true nature of her feelings?

* * *

The evening air was cool as Elise strolled over to Joan's cottage with her. 'On your own this evening?' Joan asked.

'Angelique is in the flat catching up

on a week's missed viewing on her iPlayer.'

'Let's indulge in a glass of wine then, shall we?' Joan asked. 'I'm more than ready for some refreshment. This new project of Seth's and mine is taking up more of my time than I realised. It's constant meetings and reports. Still it will be worth it.'

'About you and Seth,' Elise began as she sat on the patio.

'You are fine about it, aren't you?' Joan asked. 'I mean the shop is staying here and I've no intention of turfing you out of the flat, if you're worried about anything like that.'

'No, it's nothing to do with the shop.' Elise sipped her wine.

'You do like Seth don't you?' Joan's forehead was creased into an anxious frown.

'Of course — we all do and I'm so pleased for you getting married again.'

'Then it's Mark, isn't it?' Joan said softly. Elise nodded. 'You know I have no issues with you wanting to get married again, Elise if you want to follow my example. You're still young and attractive — and it's what Peter would have wanted too.'

'Can I ask you something personal?' Elise hesitated over the question. 'Did your marriage to Richard affect your feelings for Seth?'

'You're right, that is quite a personal one,' Joan said swirling her wine round in her glass.

'I'm sorry. I had no right to ask. Forget I mentioned it.'

'Elise, there's something you need to know. My marriage to Richard was a long and happy one and when I was widowed I had no thoughts of ever getting married again. In fact,' Joan went on, 'the first two times Seth asked me, I refused.'

'You turned him down twice?'

'Like you, I felt it would be disloyal. Then I began to realise that Seth is a good man, and although I had a wonderful marriage to Richard, he would have been the first to appreciate that life goes on and he would not want memories of the past to stand in the way of my future happiness. I realised how lucky I was to find love a second time and . . . well, I sort of engineered it for Seth to propose to me a third time. I'm not modern enough to do the proposing myself,' Joan said with a wry smile. 'So there you have the answer to your question . . . does it help?'

'Actually, I think it does.' Elise smiled at Joan.

The older woman's kindly face was wreathed in smiles. 'I'm sure Seth and I will have more than our fair share of differences. I'm quite independently minded and Seth can be a bit stubborn too, but then that's what makes a well-rounded relationship — a healthy exchange of views — isn't it? Besides I couldn't be doing with all that lovey-dovey stuff. I've never been like that. The occasional difference of opinion keeps the spark going in any relation-ship, I say.'

'Thank you for being so open with me,' Elise said.

'Just don't do anything in a hurry, Elise. If you're not sure about your feelings for Mark, then don't get involved. Too many people would get hurt if you got it wrong.'

'There you are.' Angie appeared at the French windows and pounced on the bottle of wine. 'Can I have a glass, too?'

'Only if you make it a spritzer,' Elise insisted. 'Otherwise you don't get any.' Elise whipped the bottle out of her hand.

'Honestly, Gran, you'll stick up for me won't you?'

'I would never come between mother and daughter,' Joan said, 'and I happen to think your mother is right.'

'Where's the rebel in you?' Angie squirted soda water onto the small amount of wine Elise had poured into her glass.

'I was never a rebel without a cause,' Joan replied.

'So what were you talking about then?' Angie demanded, changing the subject.

'The future.'

'You know,' Angie leaned back in her chair, 'we're all at different stages of our lives, aren't we? There's Gran about to get married again; hopefully I'm going to go to fashion college sometime in the future . . . and Mum . . . ?' she looked at Elise. 'What about you?'

Elise suspected the question was a guarded reference to her relationship with Mark but she deliberately chose to misunderstand her daughter. 'I shall carry on with my work at the college.'

'I mean, are you going to marry Mark?'

'Angie, dear,' Joan rebuked gently, 'that really is none of your business.'

'It's time someone banged their heads together. Mark's potty about her, you know.'

'Please, Angelique, I don't want to talk about it.'

223

'Rosamund Strong has moved on to pastures new. Cherry was telling Kyle she's taken up with some financier. Seriously, Mum,' Angie leaned forward, 'it's totally cool with me if you want to go ahead and get married. You could have a double wedding with Gran, now that would be something!'

'I think, young lady,' Joan stood up, 'you've done enough interfering for one night. I don't know about you but I have a full day ahead of me tomorrow so I intend having an early night.'

'Me too.' Elise stood up, ruffling Angie's hair. 'I do love you, you know.'

'Mum,' she protested half-heartedly then in an impulsive gesture leapt to her feet and kissed her mother and Joan. 'Sometimes you know, I think I'm the luckiest girl in the world.'

'Looks like we got something right,' Elise whispered to Joan as they watched Angie begin texting one of her friends about their plans for the coming week.

'Don't forget what I said,' Joan squeezed Elise's arm, 'and if things get too much for you I'm always a shoulder to cry on.'

'I don't know why mother-in-laws get such a bad press,' Elise smiled at Joan. 'You have to be the best one in the world. Come on, Angelique. Time to go.'

Still texting, Angie waved at Joan, then linking her free arm into Elise's the two of them made their way back to the flat.

14

Joan finally closed the shop door after the last browser had left for the day. 'I've never known it so busy,' she said. 'Those workmen certainly like their sandwiches doorstep style and I've handed out that many brochures, I'll have to order a reprint before stocks completely run out.'

'You do too much,' Elise chided her. 'You should delegate.'

'Character fault, I'm afraid,' Joan smiled. 'I've always been a bit of a control freak, either that,' she amended, 'or I can't help poking my nose in.'

'Why don't you have a break away somewhere with Seth?'

'During the cricket season?' Joan raised her eyebrows.

'Sorry,' Elise apologised, 'I wasn't thinking.'

'It's been as much as I could do to

get him to agree to a honeymoon, and then he insisted it was no longer than a week and before you ask our destination is a secret. You see I do know how to step back sometimes.'

'I'm pleased to hear it.'

Elise emptied the last of that day's baking out of the fresh cabinet. 'Two currant buns and one walnut and raisin loaf.'

'Is that all?' Joan shook her head. 'You'd better take them now. I wouldn't put it past one of those workmen to come back and start banging on the door if he realised he and his crew hadn't totally emptied my shelves.'

'How are things coming along?' Elise asked as she put the bread and buns on a tray.

'Haven't you been down to have a look?'

'There hasn't really been time. The first batch of students is due to arrive shortly and the college is as busy as the cricket club,' Elise replied with a twinkle in her eye.

'You've never really taken to our national game, have you?' Joan retaliated.

'Why do so many men stand in a field to play a game?'

'Pitch, dear, and they stand on it, not in it.'

'Whatever, at the end of the day they announce a draw and everyone goes home for tea. Now, boules, there's a national game I should introduce to this country.'

'I hope that was a joke.' Joan pulled down the last of the blinds. 'I'll just go and see to the animals. Are you going out tonight?' Joan held up a hand. 'I only want to know if Angie's coming over for supper.'

'Mark said he might ring, but there hasn't been a call for me, has there?'

'The telephone's only rung once today and it was Gary.'

'Maureen's son? What did he want?' Elise asked.

'I've appointed him as a permanent Saturday boy.'

'What?'

'You'd be amazed at the change in him after all that business with the donkeys and the cricket club. Maureen has more or less taken over the vegetable deliveries for me, too — it was all getting a bit too much.'

'Maureen I can understand, but Gary? He can barely string two words together to make a sentence.'

'He's just shy, that's all,' Joan replied.

'Hi, Mum, Gran.' Angie grabbed one of the currant buns before Elise could stop her. 'Did I hear Gary's name?'

'Your grandmother has offered him some Saturday work.'

'Great, that means I'll get to see him more often.'

'Excuse me?' Elise stared at her daughter in shock. 'Did I hear you right? We are talking about Gary Jenkins?'

'That's right. He's saving to go to art college. Have you seen his work? It's terrific! He's helped me design my portfolio for my fashion project.'

'What about Kyle?' Elise demanded.

'What about him?' Her hand hovered over the second bun.

'I thought you were friends.'

'We are, but like you and Mark, you know, no commitments?'

Before Elise could apprehend her daughter she whisked the remaining bun off the plate and headed towards the stairs.

Joan beamed at the confusion on Elise's face.

'I shall never understand how these things work with young people,' she complained. 'Is it me?'

'A little while ago you were complaining that you didn't want your daughter to get involved romantically and now you're at a loss to understand why she isn't. Besides, isn't everyone's love life complicated? Not that Angie's got one I hasten to add.'

Elise stared down at the small walnut loaf on her tray. It looked rather sad on its own and Elise knew exactly how it felt. Mark had promised he would be in touch but she had heard nothing from him since her visit to his new house. It was beyond her pride to contact him again. The ball was in his court if he wanted to take up her offer of a dinner date.

'See you in the morning,' Joan trilled, picking up her keys. 'Don't wait up for me. I'm off out with Seth.'

Elise heard the murmur of voices outside the shop. Before she could wonder who Joan was talking to, the doorbell rang.

'We're closed,' she said in exasperation. Her feet ached after standing all day and all she wanted to do was indulge in a hot bath then a relaxing night in.

'I've not come to stuff an aubergine,' a familiar voice replied.

'Mark?'

'Hello,' he smiled at her. 'Had a hard day?'

Elise looked down at the stained overall she was wearing. She knew her hair could do with a wash and her fingernails were severely dirt engrained from filling countless bags of potatoes.

'I . . . er,' she cleared her throat, 'since you ask, yes.'

'So it's no good telling you I've got the night off and that I could be persuaded to take you out to dinner?'

All thoughts of an early night fled. 'I thought I invited you.'

'We can argue about who pays later,' he smiled.

'What about your investigation?'

'Tell you all about that later, too.' Mark looked at his watch. 'Pick you up at eight?'

'Where are you going?' Angie asked.

'Mario's.' She whistled under her breath and Mark asked, 'What are you going to wear?'

'I don't know . . . '

Elise began a frantic search of her wardrobe once Mark had gone. She'd been out with Mark many times before but tonight she felt as nervous as a teenager on a first date.

'Is there time to wash my hair?' she asked Angie.

'Run your bath, Mum, and I'll fix you up an outfit that will have Mark unable to keep his hands off you.'

'Darling, please,' Elise complained, then giggled. 'Very well, but remember all I've taught you — understated elegance.'

'Yeh, sure,' Angie replied before diving into the back of her mother's wardrobe.

Mark was ten minutes late and Elise began to wish she hadn't gone to so much trouble with her appearance.

'Do you think I look all right?' she asked her daughter for the twentieth time in as many minutes. 'Not too much?'

'The classic little black dress, pearls topped off with a funky neck scarf, your hair freshly shampooed and your nails beautifully devoid of potato dirt. What's not to like?'

Elise held onto her clutch bag. 'This is silly, I'm so nervous.'

'Mum, you look good enough to eat and here comes Mark now.' Angie peered out of the window. 'No, you stay here for exactly . . . ' she glanced at her watch, ' . . . five more minutes.'

'Darling, isn't that rather rude? I mean, I am ready.'

'It's called playing the waiting game and I'm in charge of the rules. Now give me a twirl — I want to make sure your back looks as good as your front.'

Suddenly, Elise put a hand to her mouth, and gasped. 'Oh! I've just remembered, I can't go out tonight! Your grandmother is out too.'

'No worries. I called Gary. He's coming over and he's promised to keep me company until you get back, so you'd better not be too late or we'll come looking for you. Now remember, don't come downstairs for five minutes.'

'Mrs Trent.' Gary was with Mark and Angie in the sitting room clutching a large canvas of drawings. 'I hope you don't mind? Angie said we could look through some of our sketches.'

Elise blinked at the boy. He hardly seemed the same person who had shuffled through the shop a few weeks ago. His hair was neatly cut and he was wearing a clean T-shirt and jeans.

'Please,' she insisted, 'call me Elise and, no I don't mind. Now, you have the number of Mario's don't you? So if you're worried about anything . . .'

'That's okay, Mum said she would pop by later, Mrs — er . . . Elise,' Gary said shyly. 'She's cooking a casserole and she always makes too much, so she'll bring some round.'

'Come on, Elise,' Mark sounded impatient. 'Our table is booked for eight and we're already late. I'm sure the young people are capable of looking after themselves for a few hours.'

It was Elise's turn to feel overcome with shyness. Mark was wearing a suit, a crisp white shirt and a discreet blue tie. Elise realised she hadn't seemed him dressed so formally before and she liked his style.

'Go on, Mum, and remember what I said about behaving yourself,' Angie giggled.

'Angelique, really!'

With a firm hand under her elbow, Mark guided her outside.

'I thought we decided on a teenager free evening,' he said as he opened the passenger door for her.

'We did, and they're not coming with us.'

'Thank goodness for that. For a moment back there I thought you were going to insist they did.'

'What's Kyle doing this evening?' Elise asked.

'Hm?' Mark started up the engine. 'He's out somewhere with Cherry I think. Why?'

'You don't mind that he and Angie are no longer so close?'

'Of course not. They're only kids. None of these relationships are serious. It's part of growing up, that's all.'

* * *

Mario's was set in luxurious grounds of what was originally a Jacobean country house. In its heyday it had played host to all the important social and political families of the time. It had hosted numerous balls and diplomatic receptions and there was even a rumour that royalty had graced the house. Then after a series of disastrous investments by a profligate younger son it had lost its glamour and begun to decay.

It had finally fallen into ruin after the Second World War when troops had been billeted on the premises. They had not treated the house with the respect it deserved and after they moved out they left it a shell of its former glory.

For years it had lain unloved and untouched until a City entrepreneur with an eye to a quick turn round on his investment had purchased the property from the sole remaining heir to the family who, living in Australia, had no interest in taking up residence. The entrepreneur had carried out major refurbishment with no expenses spared, then sold it on to an up and coming restaurateur.

All this Elise had read about when looking for places of interest to take the French students during their holidays.

'Why do I feel so nervous?' Elise voiced her fears out loud as they drove through the wrought iron gates.

'Because we're doing things in style?' Mark raised an eyebrow. 'Have you noticed, not a candy floss stick in sight?'

'I shouldn't be feeling like this, Mark.'

Inadvertently she put a hand on his knee. The firm feel of his flesh under her fingertips only served to increase her nerves.

'Relax. The headwaiter assures me he's booked us the best table in the house and if you don't like what's on the menu they'll do requests within reason. How's that for service?'

'Goodness, when I suggested dinner out, I had no idea you would go to such lengths.'

'There's a lot about me you still

don't know,' Mark said.

'Is it a special occasion?' Elise did her best to keep her voice steady. 'Do we have something to celebrate?'

'Here we are.' Mark ignored her question as they drew up outside the front of the house.

A uniformed valet relieved Mark of his keys and drove the car away to a secure parking area.

The entrance hall fully lived up to its description. A huge chandelier of elegant crystal glass sparkled in the centre and every alcove was discreetly lit and filled with fresh flowers.

Elise caught her breath. Apart from the flowers and the chandelier the reception area had not been ruined by acres of expensive carpets or fiddly furniture and fittings. The decor appealed to her minimalist sense of taste and she stood still for a few moments in order to absorb the hall's elegance and style.

'Mr Hampson?' A waiter appeared. 'Mrs Trent?'

Elise turned at the sound of her name.

'Have you been here before?' she hissed in Mark's ear.

'Only once,' Mark said, a smile tugging at the corner of his mouth, 'And in answer to your question, no, it was not with Rosamund Strong.'

'I never even mentioned her name,' Elise protested.

'No, but you wanted to, didn't you?'

Elise blushed deeply; Mark had developed an uncanny instinct for reading her thoughts.

'If you didn't come with Rosamund, who did you come with?'

'Two police constables and a security consultant,' Mark replied. 'It was a professional visit to introduce myself and advise on the best way to keep the property protected,' he added. 'Luckily my security expertise, such as it is, has been more successful at Mario's than it has been at Hay Hall. Now, are you ready to go in, or would you prefer to sit on the terrace for ten minutes?'

'The terrace I think,' Elise replied, feeling the need to regain her composure for what could be a stimulating evening. They followed the waiter through the dining room and out onto the terrace where several other diners were enjoying the evening air.

'Is everything going well at the farm shop?' Mark asked as they settled down.

'Joan is more busy than ever. Now the developers have got the green light, business is booming. The workers love her home bakery range and there's a constant queue at the bread counter, not to mention the visits from potential twitchers — that is what you call bird watchers isn't it?'

'It is indeed.'

'They've read about the new development and are eager to put their names down for the cabins.'

'They're keen — it'll be at least a year surely before things are up and running?'

'What about you?' Elise leaned forward.

A waiter created an interruption with their drinks and it was several moments before Mark replied. 'Things are much the same as when I last saw you. I haven't unpacked and we're still no nearer finding the people behind the antique clocks ring.'

Elise sipped her fruit juice. 'You're not being moved on?'

'Things are very much in limbo at the moment,' Mark replied. 'I hope I'll be able to stay until Kyle has taken his exams. With Amanda living in Spain now it's more important than ever that he has a stable background.'

'My daughter tells me he has been seeing a lot of Cherry Wainwright,' Elise ventured.

'And Kyle tells me Angie is seeing a lot of Gary Jenkins,' Mark replied. 'It looks as though our comfortable little family unit is being split up, doesn't it? Time for us all to go in our separate directions?'

'I'm not moving, for the time being anyway,' Elise insisted. 'Like you, I need to stay put, at least until Angelique has had her interview for the fashion college.'

'Sorry,' Mark apologised when his mobile phone rang. 'It's me. I should have turned it off but it's my personal number and only a few people know it. I'll have to take the call.'

He stood up and moved away from their table. Elise watched him bend his head as he tried to hear what the caller was saying, then realising his private life was none of her business she turned her attention back to the rose garden.

'We're going to have to leave.'

Elise started in surprise. She had not heard Mark return to the table. 'What? Why? Has something happened?'

'That was Kyle.'

'Is he all right?' Elise demanded.

'He's fine. He's been to see a film with Cherry and he was walking her back to Hay Hall when this huge car came bowling along the lane and almost knocked them off their feet.'

'Has he been hurt?' Elise was now

seriously alarmed.

'He's fine but Cherry's hurt her leg and Kyle's called an ambulance,' he replied. 'There's something else,' Mark said as the valet hurried off to fetch his car.

'What?' Elise jumped into the passenger seat almost before the valet stopped.

Mark was already driving away as he said, 'Kyle recognised the car. He's good with things like that. He says it had the same number plate as the one that was seen outside Hay Hall on the day of the burglary.'

15

As they rounded the corner they could see blue lights flashing against the night sky. Feeling sick in the pit of her stomach, Elise, recognising the tall silhouette standing by the roadside, ran towards Mark's son and enveloped him in a bear hug as if he were still a child.

Kyle trembled in her arms and allowed her to croon words of comfort into his ear. Mark cast a glimpse in their direction, realised this wasn't the moment for paternal interference, and left Elise to comfort his son while he tried to find out exactly what had happened.

'Where's Cherry?' Elise eventually asked in a soft voice as she stroked stray locks of hair away from Kyle's face.

'The paramedics are looking after her,' he replied in a gruff voice full of embarrassment, already regretting his show of weakness. 'Over there.' He pointed to the ambulance.

Mark was now standing by the emergency vehicle speaking to a uniformed man wearing a high visibility jacket.

'What are they waiting for?'

'Mr and Mrs Wainwright haven't arrived yet. I called them after I called Dad. I'm sorry I messed up your evening,' Kyle said with a smile that was now more shy than embarrassed.

'That doesn't matter in the least,' Elise brushed aside his apology. 'How badly hurt is Cherry?'

'I think she's more shaken up than anything else,' Kyle informed her. 'She scraped her leg on a loose branch and got a bit hysterical. I didn't know what to do with her . . . wish it had been Angie,' he said.

'Excuse me?' Elise was not sure she'd heard him correctly.

'Sorry, that came out wrong . . . I mean if Angie had wound up in the hedge she wouldn't have made such a fuss. Cherry's a bit of a drama queen, but Angie would have been hurling abuse at the car driver and insisting I go get 'em.'

'All the same,' Elise bit down a smile. In her experience she had to agree with Kyle's assessment; that was exactly what her daughter would have been doing. Angie was no shrinking violet. 'It must have been a very nasty experience for Cherry and you.'

'I'm okay,' Kyle insisted, still looking a little shamefaced. 'Nothing really happened. The medics wanted me to get in the ambulance with Cherry for a check up but I wasn't having any of that — Cherry would start getting all clingy and stuff.'

Elise bit her lip. Kyle obviously didn't go for the Sir Galahad school of charm.

'Well, as long as you feel all right.' She gave him another hard look.

'I do, but thanks for coming,' he mumbled, 'apart from Mum, you're the next best person to have around.'

Elise squeezed his arm gently; she could think of no greater compliment from a boy of Kyle's age.

'Did Dad tell you I recognised the car that pushed us off the road?' Kyle asked excitedly.

'There are more important things than the identity of the car at stake,' Elise berated him.

Kyle seemed totally together, but Elise knew shock could have a different effect on people and his reaction to the incident could also be delayed.

'Cherry leapt into the hedge when the car came bowling along — that's how she came to have the scratches on her arms and legs. I think it's her dignity that's suffered more than anything else, actually.' There was an impish expression on Kyle's face. 'She has a colourful vocabulary, too — not as ladylike as we all thought. Anyway, that's why she didn't notice the number plate — but I did,' he added.

The sound of another car arriving drew their attention back to the road. Almost immediately it stopped, Rosamund Strong jumped out of the driver's seat and ran over to throw her arms around Mark's neck.

'Mark! What happened? Have you been injured? When Charles told me about the accident I was in total shock and insisted on coming over with him and Daphne.'

Kyle gave Elise a quick sideways glance, and for a moment he looked so like his father it tore at her heart, then very slowly he winked at Elise and in a man of the world voice he said, 'Can't wait to see Dad get out of this one, can you?'

'I thought you said she'd gone off with a City type,' Elise lowered her voice, anxious not to be overheard.

'She did. Dad was having terrible trouble getting rid of her actually and was well chuffed when this financial wizard appeared on the scene.'

Elise gaped at Kyle, not sure she had heard him correctly.

'You look like a goldfish,' he teased her.

'Hello, there, young Kyle isn't it?' Commander Wainwright sauntered over to join them. 'How do you do?' he shook Elise's hand. 'Not sure who you are, but thanks for all your help with my granddaughter.'

'This is Elise Trent, Commander Wainwright. Surely you remember? She's Angie's mother.'

'Of course. I thought the face was familiar.'

'It's Kyle you have to thank, not me,' Elise insisted. 'I've done nothing. It was Kyle who called the emergency services.'

'Then my wife and I are in your debt, young man,' Charles Wainwright said. He glanced over his shoulder. 'Want me to untangle Rosamund from your father? She seems to have got the wrong end of the stick. She can be a bit awkward at times.'

'Dad'll cope,' Kyle replied.

'She insisted on coming along with us and I couldn't really say no. Daphne's with Cherry in the ambulance I think. I'd better go and check things out.'

Charles Wainwright bustled off leaving Elise and Kyle still standing by the hedge.

'You were about to tell me about the French car?' Elise prompted Kyle.

'That's right. You remember the day of the summer fair? I was round the back of the kitchens,' Kyle stopped short then with a look of anguish said, 'Promise you won't tell Dad?'

'Were you smoking?' Elise demanded. Her college office overlooked the car park and many a time she had seen the students bunched together engaged in their anti-social activity.

'Not really,' Kyle mumbled. 'The others were. I went along with them that was all, but that's why I noticed the car with French number plates — because I'd wandered away from everyone else so they wouldn't notice I wasn't smoking.'

'Have you told your father this?' Elise asked him.

'Not yet — I haven't had the chance,' he replied.

Finally managing to extricate himself from Rosamund's clutches, Mark strode towards his son. Serious faced he listened to the boy's account of exactly what had happened.

'You're absolutely sure about the number?'

'Course I am. I'm good with figures. That's why I want to join the force. Do you think you could have another word with Mum? At least persuade her to let me take the exams?'

'Now's not the time,' Mark said, extricating his telephone from his coat pocket.

'I wonder why they were back in the area,' Elise mused, 'If it was the same gang, that is.'

'Where better?' Mark replied. 'No one would suspect they would return to the scene of their last crime. Pete?' Mark turned away as his call was answered.

Kyle ambled off to talk to the ambulance men, leaving Elise to face Rosamund.

'So,' she said sharply, 'you were having dinner with Mark?'

'How did you know?' Elise asked.

Rosamund raised an eyebrow as if to indicate that there was very little she didn't know about Mark's activities.

'Did you go to Mario's?'

'I take it that's where Mark took you?' Elise asked.

'He wanted to but, to be honest, I find such places a little too ornate for my taste. I always suggested somewhere with a little more understated elegance.'

Elise suspected Rosamund was being a mite economical with the truth — Mario's was exactly her sort of place.

'It is such a shame when work interrupts your dates?'

'We were interrupted by a call from Kyle, actually,' Elise replied dryly.

Rosamund dismissed the reply with an airy wave of her hand. 'Look at Mark now, so engrossed in his work, he doesn't have eyes for either of us. That's why I decided our relationship was going nowhere. I'd suggest you should do the same. Men don't like clinging females.'

'I have no intention of clinging to Mark, as you put it.'

As if sensing they were talking about him Mark turned and looked in their direction.

'I have to go. My sister needs me,' Rosamund said with a toss of her head.

Leaving behind a waft of her expensive perfume Rosamund joined the throng of people surrounding the ambulance.

'I've arranged for a traffic alert to be put out,' Mark explained. 'We had the vehicle details on file from the last time, so if the car is in the area we should be able to trace it.' He frowned. 'I only hope Kyle was right in his suspicions.'

'I'm sure he was,' Elise insisted. 'He has an eye for detail.' She paused and then added, 'Rosamund seemed very pleased to see you . . . '

Mark raised his eyes. 'Do you think . . . ' he cleared his throat awkwardly, 'that . . . er, you could do me a favour?'

'What sort of favour?' Elise asked, enjoying the look of discomfort on Mark's face.

'Would you pretend that we're together again?'

'Pretend?'

Mark cast an uneasy quick glance over his shoulder. 'The thing is, Rosamund seems to have got it into her head that we're . . . you know . . . '

'No, I don't know. You'll have to spell it out for me, Mark.'

'I saw you talking to Kyle, Elise. Didn't he tell you about me and Rosamund?'

'He was slightly less than gallant when he intimated that you were quite pleased when she began dating a financier.'

'I was,' Mark insisted, 'but there's a rumour doing the rounds that she's back in circulation. Did you see her just now?'

'With her arms flung around your neck, you mean?' Elise nodded. 'Yes, I saw her.'

'It was more than a bit embarrassing. I mean this isn't the time or the place . . . '

'In that case . . . ' Elise delivered her most winning smile as she linked an arm through Mark's and spoke to him with a loud and purringly seductive tone. 'Darling, that really is a wonderful suggestion — dinner at Mario's again next week to make up for tonight being interrupted? You really are too good to me.'

'Do what?' Mark almost spluttered.

'If you don't want to give the game away,' Elise was aware of how pronounced her French accent was in times of stress, and for a second her knowledge of English almost deserted her. 'C'est impossible. Rosamund, she comes this way. Pretend you are madly in love with me.'

'I can do better than that,' Mark leaned in towards Elise and, before she realised his intention, he very carefully, very efficiently and in full view of all those present, kissed Elise full on the lips.

'Did that do the trick, do you think?' His breath was warm against Elise's cheek and the brush of his lips against skin sent shivers up her spine.

'Everyone's looking,' she tried to protest.

'Wasn't that the idea?' It was Mark's turn to look innocent. 'I mean if I'm supposed to be madly in love with you, isn't a kiss in order?'

'Yes, but . . . '

'In that case — and in order to ensure Rosamund really does get the message . . . ' Mark's lips descended on Elise's again before she had time to protest.

The pressure of Mark's hand in the small of her back ensured she could not wriggle out of his grasp and, whilst wild horses would not have dragged the admission out of her, Elise had to admit she didn't want to move out of his hold.

'Cool it, Dad!' Through a haze of emotions, Elise heard Kyle add, 'Rosamund's stomped off, so you can

come up for air now! For goodness'
sake, put Elise down — it's embarrassing! Just wait until I tell Angie what
her mother gets up to when she goes
out with you.'

16

Sitting at her office desk at the language college the next morning, Elise was finding it difficult to concentrate on her work. The forms in front of her were a jumbled mass of words. Her head was still reeling from recent events and she'd had a sleepless night trying not to think about Mark . . .

He had driven her home after Charles and Daphne Wainwright had decided Cherry needed no more than a bit of tender loving care and the ambulance was dismissed.

With Kyle sprawled across the back seat, conversation between Mark and Elise had been stilted. Although Kyle had been busy texting his friends to update them on the latest events, Elise didn't doubt his ears were attuned to the slightest nuance in conversation between her and his father.

The tension between them had been so tight, Elise was surprised Mark had been able to concentrate on his driving. Had their kiss affected him as much as it had her?

She couldn't tell anything from his expression. In the face of Kyle's teasing she had expected Mark to rebuke his son, but instead he'd merely smiled with good-natured tolerance and told Kyle he hoped he would behave like a gentleman and not bandy around Elise's good name.

The two had smiled in a male bonding way, leaving Elise at a loss as to how to deal with her pent up emotions.

With the briefest of goodbyes, Mark had driven off after dropping Elise back at Trents Farm. Kyle had waved casually out of the passenger window as he took her place in the front seat then returned his attention to his mobile phone.

Angie had greeted her as Elise climbed the stairs to the flat that night.

'Hey, Mum — you're back early.'

To Elise's surprise it had looked as though she and Gary were still studying. The table was littered with paperwork and Angie was stretched out on the floor, surrounded by what looked like fashion designs. 'Have a good time?'

As briefly as possible Elise had acquainted them with the facts and left an excited Angie and Gary discussing what could possibly have happened and how they both agreed with Kyle that Cherry loved to be the centre of attention and was probably no more than badly scratched.

Soaking in a warm bath, Elise had tried to forget the feeling of Mark's lips on hers as she tried to convince herself the action had been purely for the benefit of Rosamund Strong, who had driven off without a backward glance.

* * *

As Elise now chewed the top of her pen, she hoped she could trust Kyle's discretion not to make too much of the incident. Regard for his father's feelings might temper his description of all that occurred. With his eye for detail Elise also hoped he might limit his story to the vehicle side of things.

With a sigh, Elise turned her attention to the latest batch of applicants for the summer school.

What she needed was routine and some sort of order in her life. Daydreaming about Mark Hampson's kisses was not what she was getting paid for.

* * *

'Have you heard the latest?' Joan greeted Elise as she arrived back home that evening.

'What's happened now?' Elise's head ached from all her close paperwork. 'Not another break in?'

'It's been on the local news. The police had a tip-off regarding the antique thefts and they've apprehended the people responsible.'

'Kyle will be over the moon,' Elise enthused.

'What's it got to do with Kyle?' Joan looked puzzled.

'It's a long story,' Elise said, remembering she hadn't had a chance to tell Joan all that had occurred the previous evening. 'Why don't you come up for a cup of tea and I'll fill you in on developments?'

'There's Seth.' Joan glanced out of the window at the sound of car tyres. 'Sorry, you'll have to tell me all about it later.'

'You're going out?'

'We've decided on a July wedding, if that's all right with you?'

'You know it is.'

'We're going to have a word with caterers about the evening's entertainment. We thought we would operate an open house policy, then people could drop in to the reception at will. There'll be plenty of scope for dancing for the youngsters and they can always spill out onto the lawn if the weather is warm.'

A disturbance from the rear of the shop reminded Joan that Maureen was still on the premises.

'Maureen and I can lock up. Off you go,' Elise urged her.

'Don't forget our date, by the way,' Joan said as she snatched up her bag and briefly inspected her reflection in the mirror. 'Heavens I'm going to have to get my hair done before the big day.'

'What date?' Elise demanded, worried that in all the fuss she had forgotten something.

'Outfits for the wedding? You remember we were going to have a girls' day out? I want Angie to be my attendant. Bridesmaid doesn't sound quite right, does it, for someone of my advanced years?'

'It will be your day, Joan, you must do as you please.'

Joan's blue eyes twinkled back at Elise. 'I haven't been this excited for years. Ridiculous, isn't it?'

'Beech Mead could do with a good

party. It will be the social event of the summer. You know, I'm sure if I had a word with Chris Saunders we could get some sort of donation towards the costs from the developers.'

'Elise!' Joan looked shocked and said, 'I'm not sure I want that at all.'

'Why not? I'm sure they'll want to be involved. They want to integrate into the community, so what better occasion could there be than the marriage of two of its most well-liked and respected citizens?'

'You always did have a good business head on your shoulders, Elise!' Joan laughed. 'I'll leave that side of things to you, then, and the fashion side to Angie. I'm sure with her sense of style she'll pick out something stunning for us all to wear.'

'Don't you think you ought to be going, Joan?' Maureen urged her as she emerged from the storeroom clutching various cardboard boxes. 'Seth is looking a bit impatient, so I'll close up for you.'

'I'm sure there was something else I had to tell you, Elise,' Joan said, frowning.

'It can wait,' Elise insisted. 'Off you go.'

'Oh! I've just remembered,' Joan poked her head back through the door just as Maureen attempted to lock it behind her. 'You will give me away, won't you?' she asked Elise. 'Coming,' she turned and waved at Seth who, running out of patience, began hooting his horn. 'All right, Seth. There's no need to blow a gasket!'

Maureen and Elise looked at each other in silence for a few moments after Seth had hurriedly driven out of the car park.

'Did I hear correctly?' Elise asked.

'Joan wants you to give her away?' Maureen replied.

'I thought that was what she said.'

'I think it's a great honour.'

'I would have thought she would have asked her sister's husband, or perhaps Seth's son.'

'Well, she didn't. She asked you.' Maureen's homely face was wreathed in smiles. 'And I think it's a lovely idea. It doesn't have to be a man, you know. Anyway you were married to Joan's son, so really, you're sort of taking his place at the ceremony, aren't you?'

With Maureen's happy chatter ringing in her ears, Elise climbed the stairs to the flat.

'By the way,' Maureen called after her, 'Angie and Gary are doing some project work at our house tonight. Harry will drive Angie home later, if that's all right with you? I can give them both supper, so you can have a nice quiet evening on your own.'

*   *   *

After Maureen left, the flat seemed very empty. Elise looked with distaste at her bulging briefcase. There was plenty of overtime on offer at the college and she had brought some work home, but despite the lack of distraction and the

267

perfect opportunity it created to catch up on her backlog she just couldn't settle.

She would have welcomed an interruption or someone to talk to, but lately everyone seemed to be going their own way. Ever since the announcement of her engagement Joan had not been around so often and there had been less shared fish stew suppers. Angie, too, seemed to have thrown herself back into her studies with renewed vigour, which left Elise with more time on her hands than she was used to.

She turned on the television and saw on the news that the police had indeed apprehended a vehicle displaying French number plates at one of the ferry ports and, although information was scarce, she was certain it had to be the car that Kyle had said sent him and Cherry into the hedge.

At first she didn't hear the downstairs bell ring. It was unusual for callers to use the shop entrance at this time of an evening and Elise's first inclination was to ignore it, then realising it could be important, she glanced out of the flat window.

Mark's car was parked outside.

'Sorry,' he apologised as he looked up and saw Elise. 'Pressed the wrong bell by mistake. Can I come in?'

Seated in the kitchen Mark nursed a mug of coffee and bit hungrily into a slab of fruitcake.

'This is good, thanks. I haven't had a chance to eat anything since breakfast.'

'Is it true?' Elise demanded as she looked into his tired face. He hadn't shaved and there were dark circles under his eyes. 'You've caught the burglars?'

'I can't tell you much about it yet, I'm afraid, but we've made a significant breakthrough. After Kyle's tip-off we were able to set up a watch on the ports and the car responsible was identified and stopped. Needless to say the number plates it displayed were false, but there was sufficient evidence to pull the drivers in for questioning.

'Bearing in mind your involvement I thought you'd like to know. Kyle, of course, is over the moon and going around telling everyone of his involvement. He's virtually taking credit for the whole operation!'

'I can imagine,' Elise laughed.

'His mother is not too pleased.' Mark made a face. 'I've had her on the telephone expressing her displeasure.'

'Isn't she proud of her son?'

'That goes without saying, but I think she'd been hoping he wouldn't follow in my footsteps. She now realises it's a hopeless cause. All Kyle wants to do is pass the entrance exams.

'I told Amanda we have to play to his strengths and I think she's coming round. I hope so anyway, because it would be a shame to deny Kyle the one thing he wants to do in life.'

Elise resisted the urge to reach out and squeeze Mark's fingers. Everything was going so well for them both and she was really pleased, but shared intimacies were not on the agenda, despite the closeness of their embrace the night before.

'Cherry's fine by the way,' he added. 'I've also had Rosamund on the telephone.'

'You have?' Elise asked with a sinking of her heart.

'Yes.' Mark helped himself to another slice of cake. 'She wanted to say goodbye.'

'She is leaving?'

'She's got some sort of consultancy work in London she said, and now Charles and Daphne are getting settled in at Hay Hall, she's decided it's time to move on.'

'That is good news,' Elise spoke without thinking, then flushed at the intensity of the look Mark subjected her to.

'You think so, too?'

'Of course — I mean, for you. This latest development also means you won't be moving out of the area now, won't it?' Elise decided to deliberately misinterpret his question. 'Kyle will be able to stay at college and you can settle in your new house.'

'Time for new beginnings all round, then?'

'Exactly.'

'Thank you for all your help last night by the way.' The suggestion of a smile curved Mark's lips. 'I'm not sure how much of an influence our actions had on Rosamund's decision to take up her consultancy but whatever, it seems to have done the trick.' Mark finished his coffee. 'I have to get home now, I'm afraid — I promised Kyle an evening at the stock car racing.'

Mark stood up, then paused. 'We may have to put our next dinner date on hold for a while. Work schedules are all over the place at the moment, what with all this latest business.'

'I understand.'

'That's the trouble with being a policeman's wife — not that you are one, but you know what I mean.'

Mark leaned forward and kissed her on the cheek. 'I'll be in touch,' he promised. 'Bye.'

Elise put a hand to her face on the spot where his lips had touched her cheek. It had been no more than a friendly embrace, but yet again the feel of Mark's lips on her skin had left her senses tingling.

17

The oyster pink dress and matching jacket, topped with an outrageous cartwheel hat, totally transformed Joan's image as she inspected her reflection in the changing room mirror.

'No peeping at the price tag,' Angie informed her sternly as she made a few unnecessary adjustments to the fit across Joan's shoulders.

'What do you think, Elise?' Joan asked.

Elise peered through the curtains, her breath catching in her chest. 'I have never seen you look so glamorous,' she replied.

'She has to have it doesn't she, Mum?' Angie insisted. 'Chris Saunders said we were to send him the bill.'

'Yes, dear, but I'm sure he meant we were to go somewhere a little less exclusive,' Joan butted in.

'If our photos are going to feature in his summer newsletter then we must do him proud. It's all good public relations, you know, so no more of that. Right, that's Gran sorted.' Angie clapped her hands as if she were in charge of the boutique and turned to face her mother. 'Your turn, now, Mum.'

Elise hid a smile as the assistants scurried to obey her teenage daughter's command.

'Isn't this fun?' Angie flashed a dimpled smile at her mother and giggled as Joan battled with her hat.

'Don't squash it, Gran. Here let me . . . '

The two women succumbed meekly to Angie's expertise. When it came to fashion they were clearly on her territory.

For her mother, Angie had chosen a simple off white shift with a bolero jacket and pillbox hat. Elise had insisted she did not want to draw attention away from the bride's big day.

'Yes, you'll do,' Angie said briskly, stepping back and eyeing her mother's trim figure in the elegantly understated outfit. 'We'll have to do something about your hair, of course, and . . . ' Angie admonished the pair of them with a frown, ' . . . will you please not have anything to do with potatoes the week before the wedding?'

'I've been on a diet, sort of,' Joan complained, 'but I like my new potatoes this time of year.'

'You can eat them, but I don't want either of you handling them — you get dirt under your nails and it makes manicuring them very difficult.'

Joan and Elise exchanged looks.

'Have we created a monster?' Joan gum-shoed out of the side of her mouth as Angie berated one of the assistants for crushing Joan's jacket.

'Isn't she marvellous?' Elise's eyes shone with pride. 'You've got to admit, Joan, we would have been lost without her. I would never have dared to come in here. I mean, it's the most exclusive place on the south coast.'

'Yes, the young are full of confidence these days, aren't they? I would never have dared either.'

'I do hope she gets her place in fashion college. Look at her now, overseeing everything.'

'You've done your bit as well, Elise — I mean, suggesting Chris Saunders should get his bosses to contribute to the big day as a marketing exercise. That was a touch of genius.'

'That was rather clever of me, wasn't it?' Elise exchanged a conspiratorial smile with her mother-in-law. 'I really had in mind a small donation, but if they're willing to foot the fashion bill, I'm not going to argue with them.'

'Are we finished, then?' Angie turned back to the pair.

'What about you, dear?' Joan queried. 'You'll have to wear something appropriate, too.'

'Now, there I intend to surprise you,' Angie replied as, with all the assurance of youth, she signalled to a hovering attendant.

Moments later swathes of tissue paper and huge dress boxes were being produced as more assistants folded the outfits and attended to all the other details of the sale.

'I have some news for you both,' Angie said as they sat down in the padded chairs and sipped the mineral water provided by the expensive boutique.

'I hope it's good news,' Joan said, gently massaging her now very tired legs.

'The best,' Angie replied. 'Are you listening, Gran?' she demanded, seeing Joan was a little distracted.

'I'm used to being on my feet all day but these shoes are beginning to pinch. What was that, dear?'

Angie paused for dramatic effect before announcing, 'I have been offered an interview with the principal of the fashion college for a place.'

'Darling!' Elise hugged her daughter.

'That is wonderful news. Why didn't you tell us earlier?'

'I wasn't sure I'd be successful. Then . . . well, Gary promised to help me with my presentation. You know, photographs of my work, that sort of thing. Part of my remit is to design a dress of my own and I thought an attendant's dress for a summer wedding would be the perfect thing to showcase my work. We've been working on it in secret. I borrowed Maureen's sewing machine and it's nearly ready.'

'When is this interview?' Joan demanded.

'Next week.' Angie's deep violet blue eyes displayed only a hint of nervousness as she crossed her fingers. 'Wish me luck.'

'You'll pass,' Joan pronounced with certainty.

'Don't be too sure, Gran, the competition is keen.'

'Your grandmother is right,' Elise said. 'Look at the outfit you're wearing today. You have a unique style.'

279

For their trip Angie had chosen to wear a hard brimmed black hat, a vibrant striped top and crushed raspberry cargo pants. The effect was young, full of optimism and very individual. With her long, blonde hair she looked a picture of youth at its loveliest and most vibrant.

'I don't know about you two,' Joan announced, 'but I'm parched after all this. What say we have a slap-up tea at one of the big hotels on the sea front before we make our way home?' Joan nodded to the vast array of boxes that now appeared to be surrounding their exit, and asked, 'Can these be delivered?'

'But of course, madam,' the manageress smiled.

'Listen to Gran,' Angie whispered with a giggle, 'giving orders as if she was born to it.'

'There's no way we can accommodate all this in the car,' Joan told Angie, 'and I'm not having my outfit squashed on the back seat, young lady.'

Elise produced the card Chris Saunders had issued to her and it was whisked away by an ultra efficient receptionist.

'So . . . that's shoes, underwear, a going away outfit,' Angie ticked everything off on her fingers. 'I think we're done.'

'Thank goodness for that,' Joan said. 'Let's go and get some fresh air in our lungs now.'

* * *

'I hope you didn't mind,' Maureen apologised to Elise as she made her way through the shop.

'Sorry?' Elise paused, looking around for her car keys.

'About Angie using my sewing machine. I would have mentioned it to you only she swore me to secrecy.'

'Of course I don't mind,' Elise smiled.

'You should have seen them working together. My Gary is very good with a camera. Harry bought him one last Christmas and he's really taken to it. Like Angie, he's got an eye for colour and detail. If I say so myself, the pair of them are very professional, young as they are.'

Elise could not believe the change in the shy and surly youth who had gazed adoringly at her daughter only two months ago. These days he virtually ran the shop when he worked there on a Saturday. With his new-found self-confidence he was beginning to blossom and find his way in life — there seemed almost to be a spring in his step.

'It's today, isn't it?' Maureen asked in a lowered voice as if she didn't like asking the question out loud.

'Angelique's interview? Yes,' Elise nodded. 'I have such butterflies in my stomach, you cannot believe it.'

'She'll be fine,' Maureen assured her. 'Do you know she's making me a summer dress for the wedding? It's lovely, all sea green and sort of blue-y with little sleeves. I'm not very good at describing it, but even my Harry said it looked lovely. You must be so proud of her.'

'I am,' Elise smiled at Maureen, 'as you must be of Gary.'

Maureen's ruddy complexion turned a shade deeper. 'I can't tell you how glad I am things have turned out so well. When I think of all that business with the cricket club and how kind everyone has been to Harry and me and then Gary turning out so well and Joan giving me a bit more responsibility,' Maureen paused, overcome with emotion.

Elise squeezed her fingers. 'You know, my father always used to say things generally turned out well in the end, and I think he was right.'

'How are things between you and Kyle's father?' Maureen asked. Elise's expression told her the question took her by surprise. 'I'm sorry,' Maureen apologised quickly, 'I know it's not my place to ask . . . it's just that . . . well, everyone else seems to be getting their lives sorted out and I thought it might be rather nice if you and Mark . . . well, you know . . . '

It hurt Elise to smile back and pretend that all was well. Thoughts of Mark had been going through her mind but, apart from the occasional courtesy telephone call or text, there had been nothing.

Now Kyle and Angie were no longer so close their lives were not so intimately intertwined any more. Neither had there been any renewal of Mark's dinner date invitation.

'We were friends because of Kyle and Angelique,' Elise explained in what she hoped was a steady voice. 'Now your Gary and Angelique seem so friendly, we seem to have drifted apart.'

'That's a pity,' Maureen sympathised. 'The pair of you seemed so right for each other. There was a time a few months back when I thought he was really sweet on you.'

'I'm afraid I must be going,' Elise cut Maureen short.

'I'll keep my fingers crossed for Angie,' Maureen called after her as she left the shop.

Lost in her thoughts Elise did not immediately notice the figure standing in front of her.

'Hello, there. Just thought I'd pop in briefly with a good luck card for Angie.' Chris Saunders beamed at her. 'Clare has signed it too,' he explained with a laugh. 'And if she wonders what the splodge on the bottom is, it's a kiss from Molly.'

'That's very kind of you. Thank you.'

'I must say the bosses were very impressed with the dress she's going to wear for Joan's wedding. It's going to be a big feature of my next newsletter,' Chris told her. 'Anyway, best of luck — gotta go — I'm on my way to a site meeting.' He nodded towards the development. 'The planners are paying us a visit.'

He kissed Elise on the cheek. 'Lovely to see you,' he smiled. 'Perhaps we could have dinner together again some time?'

'That would be lovely.'

The sound of someone clearing their throat behind her made her jump. 'Mark?' she turned round in surprise. 'What are you doing here?'

'I also came to deliver a good luck card for Angie.'

Elise blinked at him. 'That's just what Chris was doing, too,' she explained.

'It looked to me as though he was kissing you.' Mark didn't look entirely convinced.

Why was it every time Chris kissed her on the cheek, Mark seemed to appear from nowhere? The look in his eyes suggested she had no right to be kissed on the cheek by a married man, but then what business was it of Mark's?

Elise was surprised at how angry she felt.

'It's from Kyle and me . . . for Angie . . . ' Mark explained before Elise had a chance to speak. 'Kyle meant to post it yesterday but he forgot and it completely slipped my mind too. We've been so busy sorting out the house that we're forgetting things left, right and centre.'

Elise took the brightly coloured envelope from him. 'I'll give it to her tonight.'

'Are you on your way to work?' Mark asked.

'Yes. It's forms all the time at the moment,' Elise replied, 'but I'm working from home today.'

'Kyle's been doing a fair bit of that too.'

'He is going ahead with his plans to join the police force?'

'We hope so, now he's managed to talk his mother round.'

Aware that Maureen would have a full view of them through the glass windows fronting the shop, Elise tried to subtly move out of her line of vision.

'So, how are you?' she asked, noting with a tinge of exasperation that he seemed remarkably fit.

'I've been getting to grips with the

garden when I haven't been working,' Mark explained. 'Seth has been advising me on the best vegetables to grow so I'm working on a vegetable patch at the moment.'

'Seth?' Elise repeated in surprise.

'He really knows his stuff. I didn't like to ask him at first, what with him being so busy with plans for this new community centre and the cricket club and . . . ' Mark frowned, 'I think there was something else . . . oh, yes!' His blue eyes filled with amusement, 'He's getting married . . . it's soon, isn't it?'

'Only three weeks away, now,' Elise replied.

Mark nodded. 'I mustn't keep you. Let me know how Angie gets on, won't you?'

'I will,' Elise replied as Mark strode back to his car.

She stood where she was in frustration for a few moments after he had driven off.

Why hadn't she plucked up the courage to remind him about their dinner date? Why didn't he mention it — had it slipped his mind? Mark had said he and Kyle were so busy they kept forgetting things, but surely he would have remembered the night of the accident?

Elise turned over the brightly coloured envelope Mark had given her. Perhaps, Elise thought, if Angie was successful in her college application — and after Joan's wedding — she ought to think more about setting her own life in order.

Joan would be more than busy with her new married life and Angie would be forging on with creating her own future. It was time she got herself organised, too.

★　★　★

Elise almost jumped when her mobile phone buzzed in her bag. She glanced at her watch and saw with shocked surprise that it was nearly lunchtime. Working from home this morning had taken up more of her time than she intended.

Her heart thumped loudly when she saw on the display that the caller was Angie.

'Angelique? How are you? Have you had your interview? How did it go? You must tell me everything! By the way, I have two cards for you — one from Chris and one from Kyle. Mark gave me Kyle's card in the car park. Oh, and Maureen said she was going to keep her fingers crossed for you . . .'

'Mum,' Angie implored down the line, 'slow down.'

'Sorry, darling, I am so nervous for you. What happened? Tell me every-thing, please.'

'I'm trying to. If you'll only give me a chance,' Angie's voice was full of barely suppressed excitement. 'I'm in!'

'In what?'

'Fashion college, next term! Isn't that brilliant?'

Aware of someone banging on the window behind her, Elise turned round to see Maureen almost jumping up and down in excitement. Like Elise, she was holding a mobile phone to her ear. Elise guessed that Gary must have phoned her with the good news, too.

'I am so proud of you, Angelique,' Elise said into the phone while waving happily to Maureen. 'That really is the most wonderful news.'

'I told them I was half French and that my grandmother used to work for one of the big fashion houses as a mannequin, and they really liked my work and it was absolutely terrific! I'm so excited I can hardly speak!'

'You must tell your grandmother, too,'

'I tried her mobile but she's not answering,' Angie explained. 'But if you see her don't mention it, I want to tell her myself.'

'I won't, I promise.'

'I'm off to celebrate with my friends for a while,' Angie trilled, 'I've got to go, Mum, see you tonight.'

18

Elise would have recognised Seth's son, David, anywhere. He had the same quirky smile and deep-set hazel eyes.

'I'm a vet too, like Dad was until he retired,' he informed Elise as he subjected her to a bone-crushing handshake on their first meeting.

'I didn't know that.' Elise hoped David wouldn't notice her flex her fingers when he released her.

'I suppose I must get my love of wildlife from him too. I spend days in my log cabin up in the mountains chilling out, away from it all.'

'You're not married, then?'

'I was . . . ' David hesitated, 'I'm a bit of a loner, I'm afraid, and my wife . . . well, she was a city girl, liked the bright lights. Me, I'm never happier than when I'm out in the open air communing with nature.'

'Do you have children?'

'No, but some day perhaps, who knows? And you have a daughter? Angie's a beautiful girl, isn't she?'

'I think so,' Elise replied, 'but then I am her mother, so I suppose I'm a little biased.'

'I can see from where she gets her beauty.' David gave her another of his broad smiles.

'David emigrated to Canada as a young man after my first wife died,' Seth had informed Elise earlier, 'and we don't see that much of each other. We're close, but in a male sort of way. We don't catch up often, but when we do, we take up where we left off as if we'd been apart for no more than a day. I'm hoping Joan and I will be able to visit him in Canada when things have settled down a bit. It's a beautiful country and I'm sure she would enjoy it.'

'Perhaps you could have a delayed honeymoon?' Elise had suggested to him.

As it was, and after much discussion, Joan and Seth had decided to only take a long weekend off to stay in a quiet country hotel. As it was their busiest time of the year, neither of them felt able to take any longer.

'Good suggestion,' Seth had said. 'Now, you will look after my David while he's over, won't you — introduce him to everyone? He'll be staying with me, but he doesn't know anyone and I'll be busy.'

'It will be my pleasure,' Elise had assured Seth.

David was the kind of man it was easy to relate to. With his individual brand of new world charm he didn't stand on ceremony and was perfectly prepared to pitch in at the shop or any other activity that was going. Maureen too was smitten.

'He manhandled the entire consignment of new potatoes into the store room yesterday,' she informed Elise, 'and without any help, too. And afterwards he drove Gary all the way to his photographic meeting because Harry and I were busy. He's such a gentleman. Will he be escorting you to the wedding?' she asked with a wide-eyed, innocent look on her face.

'I'll be in the car with Joan,' Elise replied, oblivious. 'David will accompany his father.'

'And later?' Maureen pushed.

'Plans are still a bit hazy at the moment. There'll be a wedding breakfast for the family, of course, but then everyone will be coming back to The Beech Mead Hotel for the party.'

'Well, if you don't mind my saying so, Elise, you could do a lot worse, you know.'

'Than what?'

'David Baxter,' Maureen said with a grin. 'He's well set up and if you were looking for a new start . . . ?'

'Which I'm not, Maureen,' Elise replied with good humour. 'And even if I were I certainly couldn't even begin to think about moving to Canada. Angelique is at a very critical stage of her life and I couldn't possibly leave her.'

'I suppose not,' Maureen agreed reluctantly. 'I don't mean to interfere, but what with Mark Hampson seemingly off the scene, it would be so nice to see you settled with someone.'

'I'm perfectly happy as I am, Maureen. I'm happy to be single,' she stressed, trying not to frown. It was only with the tightest of self-control that she was able to stop herself from adding, 'If I can't have Mark.'

* * *

The day of Joan's wedding dawned bright and warm, and by nine o'clock it was obvious it was going to be a beautiful July summer day.

The service was scheduled for half-past-eleven and Joan's cottage was a flurry of activity. The telephone rang constantly, together with the front door bell as deliveries of presents and flowers continued to arrive.

'I had no idea we knew so many

people,' Joan said happily as she was presented with yet another bouquet.

'Who's that one from?' Angie asked, finishing off her breakfast toast and marmalade.

'Chris and Clare Saunders. Aren't they beautiful? Where am I going to put them?'

'In a bucket of water for the time being, I think. Give them to me,' Maureen insisted. 'We don't want you ruining your outfit by getting pollen marks on it.'

'I haven't got it on yet,' Joan pointed out.

'Maureen's right, Gran. You're wearing your new underslip beneath your dressing gown and pollen stains are virtually impossible to get out.'

'Good heavens,' Elise gasped as she inspected another bouquet. 'You'll never guess who this one is from! Councillor and Mrs Newman.' She held the card aloft. 'And it's signed Sarah and Jack.'

'I know.' Joan's laugh was bordering

on an unladylike guffaw. 'Isn't that something else? I quite warmed to Councillor Newman, ever since he took his wife to task over that business with Gertie and their son.'

'It's no good, Gran,' Angie sighed. 'If you get any more presents, you're going to have to move house!'

'Nothing would make me leave my cottage,' Joan replied.

Angie and Elise stared at Joan in surprise and after a moment's hesitation, Elise asked, 'Then what are you going to do? Seth wants to stay in his house too, doesn't he?'

'He does and he will be for the time being,' Joan explained. 'We intend to use both the cottage and Seth's house.'

'That sounds like a very modern arrangement,' Elise said with a knowing nod. 'I approve.'

'Great,' Angie enthused. 'If you fall out you've always got somewhere else to go and you'll always keep your allure, Gran. You know, a sense of mystery?'

'Do you know what your daughter is

talking about?' Joan asked Elise. 'A sense of mystery indeed,' she tutted. 'At our age, Seth and I haven't time for that sort of thing. Our arrangement is purely practical, that's all.'

'Only teasing, Gran,' Angie said. 'Now, are you going to have the last piece of toast? You're always telling me a good breakfast sets you up for the day.'

'Just some juice, dear. My stomach is churning. Where's that manicurist?' Joan looked at her watch for the about the twentieth time in as many minutes.

'She'll be here. Chill.' Angie munched away at her toast. 'I'll need to come upstairs with you, by the way. I know you — you'll probably get nail varnish on your dress if I don't keep an eye on you.' She turned to look at Elise. 'What about you, Mum?'

'I can look after myself, Angelique, don't worry about me. It's Joan's day.'

'Here's the manicurist and the hairdresser now,' Joan said in relief as she looked out of the window.

*   *   *

Somehow everyone managed to be ready by eleven.

The beribboned car arrived on time and drove Angie to the church first.

Her dress had indeed been an inspirational creation. She had modelled it along classical Greek lines, its plain simplicity emphasising her slender young figure and Elise could see why the team from the fashion college had been impressed. It was a mature piece of work and was an excellent showpiece for Angie's talent.

Joan and Elise sat opposite each other as they waited for the car to return from delivering Angie to the church.

'The cottage seems very quiet,' Joan said wistfully.

'It's good to have these last few minutes to ourselves.'

'Have you had any more thoughts about Mark?' Joan asked carefully. 'I have no wish to pry . . . ' she added.

300

'We see each other occasionally, although mostly for professional reasons,' Elise said, 'but that isn't what you want to know, is it?'

'Tell me if it's none of my business,' Joan smiled gently, 'but are you in love with him?'

'Yes,' Elise answered simply.

The roll of tyres on the lane outside broke into the silence that had fallen between the two women.

'But when he asked me to marry him, I turned him down,' Elise said suddenly. 'And I don't think he'll ask again.'

'Don't give up hope,' Joan smiled. 'Remember what I told you about Seth.'

'For goodness' sake,' Elise smiled at her mother-in-law, 'what are we doing talking about my non-existent love life? You're getting married today! Now, come on. You've asked me to give you away, so I'd better get down to my duties.'

'Not so fast,' Joan held her back. 'It's

a bride's prerogative to arrive a few minutes late, isn't it? Let's have a sip of champagne to steady our nerves.'

'For an English woman,' Elise smiled back at Joan, 'you have some very French ideas at times. Where did you put the bottle?'

'It's on ice in the fridge.'

★ ★ ★

The look Seth gave Joan as she and Elise, fuelled by their champagne, finally walked down the aisle almost took Elise's breath away.

The atmosphere in the square Norman church was hushed as the organist began to play the wedding march. Heads turned and there in the front pew were David and Seth, smiling with identical looks of love on their faces.

Although David had only just recently met the family, they had all taken to him so well, it was as if he had always been a part of their lives.

The service was short and simple and, as Seth slipped the ring on Joan's finger and they made their vows, Elise felt tears prick the back of her eyes.

Angie squeezed her mother's fingers and they exchanged watery smiles before Elise took her place next to David behind the newly married couple.

Angie adjusted Joan's hat that had slipped a little when Seth kissed her. 'Okay,' she whispered, 'ready for the off?'

They began their dignified procession back down the aisle, acknowledging friends and relatives with happy smiles until they were all outside in the bright sunshine and the photographer marshalled them all together for the photographs.

During a brief interlude, Elise moved away from the action as Seth and Joan posed for their final photograph.

'I must congratulate you ladies on your choice of outfits.' Chris appeared at her side. He looked very smart in his morning dress. Elise had spotted Clare and an adorable looking Molly in a pink dress amongst those taking their own photographs of the happy couple.

'I was just a little scared we had gone over the top,' she said rather anxiously.

'Not at all,' Chris insisted. 'The newsletter editor will be thrilled. The front page is usually full of mundane stuff like surveys and when the next log cabin updates will be announced. A wedding will set a completely different tone.'

'My daughter was responsible, really.'

'It was a lovely ceremony wasn't it?' Angie strolled over to join them both.

'I'd better get back to my family,' Chris said. 'Well done, both of you,' he beamed before making his way back to his wife and little daughter.

'What's that?' Angie suddenly demanded. 'Over there.' She delivered a sharp blow with her elbow and Elise stumbled. Angie ducked quickly at the same time and the next moment, Elise found she was clutching the bride's bouquet.

'You engineered that,' Elise gasped, her ribs still smarting from the jab Angie had delivered. 'It was meant for you.'

She looked across to where Joan was blowing her a kiss.

'You caught it, Mum,' Angie said, having none of it. 'You saw her, David, didn't you?' She turned to him for support.

'I did indeed. Hey, does that mean I'm in with a chance? Doesn't tradition dictate that whoever catches the bouquet is going to be the next lady to get married?'

'Kyle,' Angie called over to where he was standing under a tree helping Gary take some photos. 'Did you see Mum catch Gran's bouquet?'

'Sure did.'

'David is thinking about proposing to her. What do you think of that, then?' Angie laughed.

'Don't know what Dad's going to have to say about that.'

Elise bit her tongue, determined not to spoil Joan's big day by rising to the bait. 'Will everyone please stop trying to marry me off?' she protested with a forced smile. 'I am quite happy just as I am.'

'Single and sad?' Angie queried with a wry grin.

'Don't talk nonsense!' Elise retorted.

'Be that as it may,' David butted in, 'I can think of another wedding tradition — the best man gets the first dance with the chief bridesmaid.'

'Gran didn't have one,' Angie pointed out.

'Exactly, so I should say that means I get to dance with you, Elise, wouldn't you?'

'Shouldn't you be attending to your duties as best man?' Elise replied, trying to deflect his attentions. 'You're supposed to be gathering everyone up and pointing them in the right direction for the wedding breakfast.'

'I can recognise a put down when I get one and I guess you're right about marshalling the folks,' David replied good-humouredly in his transatlantic drawl. 'I wasn't around the first time Dad got married, so I'm a bit rusty on etiquette.' He turned to face the crowd. 'Come on, folks,' he bellowed, as if he were rustling cattle, 'time to get some food!'

Elise stood where she was for a moment, after Angie had strolled off with Gary and Kyle. Joan's bouquet was a simple display of pink roses and gypsophila and as she held it in her hands, she wondered briefly what it would be like to get married again. It would mean a loss of independence and the inevitable differences of opinion, but it would also mean companionship on cold winter nights when the wind was howling around outside.

There would be someone with whom to share a summer holiday, or to enjoy a lazy day doing nothing. The bathroom would probably need more frequent cleaning and changing of towels.

Elise remembered how bad Peter had

been at doing the dishes or making the beds, but he had always been there when she needed him.

A shadow slanted across her vision, breaking into her reveries and making her look up with a start. 'Mark? What are you doing here?'

'I've come to escort you to the wedding breakfast,' he said.

'I didn't know Joan had invited you. Sorry,' she apologised, 'that sounded unforgiveably rude. I meant that I thought it was only family and a few close friends.'

'I may not be family, but I hope I can be counted as a close friend.' His eyes strayed to the flowers Elise was clutching. 'A little bit undignified, wasn't it — tussling with your daughter to catch the bride's bouquet?'

'I did not tussle with Angelique!' Elise replied indignantly. 'She jabbed me in the ribcage. I put out my arm and the next thing I knew I was holding the flowers.'

'Not a good enough excuse.' Mark

smiled down at her. 'Angie told me what really happened and I think I like her version of events better than yours.'

'And just what did my daughter tell you?'

'That it was you who pushed her.'

'At the risk of denouncing my own daughter,' Elise's cheeks grew hot with indignation, 'that is simply not true.'

'All the same, I thought I might as well lay first claim.'

'First claim?' Elise echoed faintly.

'I didn't like the way that David was constantly hovering. He was all over you like a bad rash.'

'Seth asked me to look after him, as it happens.'

'David seems more than able to look after himself,' Mark observed, then added, 'And as for Chris Saunders, he's married so he's out of the running.'

'Out of the running for what?' Elise asked.

'I was wondering if by any chance . . .' Mark paused.

A soft breeze disturbed his hair and

Elise fought down an absurd urge to straighten it.

'You turned me down once . . . ' he reminded her in a soft voice that made her feel strangely dizzy.

Above them the breeze now shook the branches of the spreading elm and Elise could smell the scent of the roses in Joan's bouquet. The sky was incredibly blue and in the distance she could hear the drone of a lawn mower somewhere.

She looked into Mark's anxious blue eyes.

'You could try asking me again,' she said slowly.

'And?'

'I won't turn you down a second time,' she admitted.

19

It was lucky that most of Beech Mead had decided to attend Joan and Seth's party as the noise from the reception was reaching pollution levels. Like Elise and Mark, many of the older folk had slipped outside, to leave the youngsters — who were showing no signs of flagging — to gyrate to the pounding beat of the disco music.

'Why do I feel so old watching the young people dance?' Elise asked Mark.

'You could never be old,' he responded gallantly with that quirky smile that Elise loved so much.

'All the same I don't think I could party all night these days.'

'Thank goodness for that,' Mark responded. 'Let's leave that sort of thing to the next generation.'

Several of the contract workers from the development had joined in the festivities and brought their families with them, much to Mark's delight.

'At last all our problems seem to be behind us,' he said as a local girl strolled along hand-in-hand with one of the carpenters who had been working on the log cabins.

'I do hope so.'

'The development has been finally settled and the perpetrators of the antiques burglaries are in custody.'

'I can't believe so much has happened in the space of a few short months,' Elise agreed. 'I can hardly keep up with events.'

They were seated on one of the garden benches, sipping chilled fruit juices and enjoying the evening air.

'You're not having second thoughts already, are you?'

'Whatever gave you that idea?' Elise asked.

Her head was still whirling. She still couldn't quite believe that Mark had proposed to her for a second time. Joan had predicted he would, and if her mother-in-law hadn't been otherwise engaged all day, Elise might have suspected her of having a hand in things.

'I suppose I can't believe you actually said yes. In April you were so adamant that you didn't want to get married again.'

'I changed my mind. It's allowed isn't it?'

'It is the prerogative of your sex,' Mark agreed. 'Can I hold your hand?' he asked, adding, 'No one's looking.'

'We had an agreement that we weren't going to upstage Joan and Seth,' Elise reminded him.

'They left half an hour ago and it's starting to get dark. I don't think anyone will notice.'

'Your fingers are cold.' Elise shivered as she felt the contrast of Mark's skin, cold against her warm hand.

'Sorry, it's the ice in the fruit juice,' Mark explained. 'But I'm not going to let go, and if you struggle people will start to wonder what we're up to.'

'You are an impossible man . . . ' Elise began.

'Are we having our first lovers' tiff?' Mark asked with an engaging smile. 'Because if we are, it's fun isn't it?'

'We are not 'tiffing', as you call it.'

'There's no such word.'

In the fading light, the lines on Mark's face softened. Every so often his complexion turned a violent hue of purple or of psychedelic yellow as the lights from the disco across the lawn exploded in their direction.

'I'm so glad David didn't come looking for you to claim the first dance,' Mark admitted, 'Otherwise, I might have had to get firm with him.'

'Rosamund saw to that,' Elise replied.

'Ah, yes, the fair Rosamund.' There was a wry twist to Mark's lips as he said her name.

'I'm sure Joan didn't invite her.'

'Joan issued an open house invitation for the reception, so technically everyone was invited — and as far as I can see, everyone came. I expect Rosamund saw no reason why she should be left out. Whatever, she and David seem to be getting along really well, don't they?'

When David had seen the look on Mark's face as he tried to approach Elise for a dance, he had turned away and bumped into Rosamund, who, also seeing Mark and Elise together, had decided to make the best of a bad job by asking David to dance.

'There really was nothing between you and Rosamund, then?' Elise asked.

'Do you want the honest truth?' Mark asked.

'Please,' Elise insisted, although with a sinking heart. 'So there was something?'

'When I first met her, I thought Rosamund might be involved in the robbery ring, actually.'

'What?' Elise's squawk disturbed the rooks in the branches above them.

'Not very gallant of me, I know, but she was high maintenance, she turned up at the right time, and she always seemed to know everything that was going on.'

'But it was her family that was burgled.'

'Stranger things have happened, Elise.'

'I cannot believe you would think such a thing.'

'Looking back, neither can I, but there you have it. I could see that she wasn't really interested in security at our meetings and that got me thinking ... Why? What was her motivation in getting me to take her out to dinner?'

'That was because she was only interested in you,' Elise forced herself to say.

'Is that why you were so jealous of her?' Mark asked.

'I was not jealous,' Elise did her best to salvage her pride. It would do no good, she decided, to let Mark continue thinking along those lines. At times he really could be impossible. 'Besides, you were the one who was jealous. Look what you did to Chris and me that day at the fair.'

'That was unfortunate,' Mark agreed, 'and I have to admit I wasn't happy about your relationship with him, especially when I found out he had a wife and baby.'

'Which I knew about all along.'

'Yes, but I didn't know you knew and these public relations people can be a bit fast and loose. I thought maybe he was feeling lonely without his family and he was using you as a sort of stop-gap.'

Twin dimples dented Elise's cheeks. 'Now who's jealous?' she goaded Mark.

He ignored her as he said, 'Then when David appeared on the scene, I knew I had to act fast if I didn't want to lose you again. I'd purposely stayed out of your way in the hope that you'd miss me. It was easier when Kyle and Angie went their separate ways, but I can't say I enjoyed it.'

'What about Amanda?'

'My ex-wife? What about her?'

'Will she mind you marrying again?'

'Not at all. We're very good friends, but she has a new husband and a new life in Spain. All she wants is for Kyle to be happy and I know he is. He likes you and he and Angie get along well too, so there's no problem there.'

'Do you know Seth had to propose to Joan three times before she accepted him?'

'Thank goodness you didn't make me do it a third time!' Mark laughed. 'I might have lost my nerve!' His hand was warmer now as he squeezed Elise's fingers. 'How much longer do we have to stay here?'

'You're not enjoying yourself?'

'Like I said, I'm a bit old for noisy parties. I hope you don't mind. I like quiet evenings in, eating fish stews made by a beautiful French woman, with perhaps a glass of wine. What could be better?'

'You won't mind if an excitable teenage daughter occasionally inter-rupts things?'

'Or a noisy teenage son? Kyle can be equally as disruptive at times.'

'I like young people. They make for vibrancy,' Elise said. 'If we want to go somewhere quiet we can always visit Joan and Seth — although I believe that they've both been a bit racy in their pasts.'

'We'll be a ready-made family unit,' Mark laughed. 'I think there might be a few problems up ahead and we could end up being piggy in the middle.'

A loud disturbance from the dance hall drew everyone's eyes towards the terrace.

'Hope it's nothing serious,' Mark said. 'I'd hate to have to get involved.'

'I think it's David,' Elise peered into the gathering gloom.

'In that case he's old enough to look after himself. What's he doing?' Mark asked. 'I daren't look.'

'It seems to be some sort of native prairie dance. He's wiggling his hips and making wolf noises.'

'In that case I'd say it's more than

time we left to go home, wouldn't you? It looks as though the rest of the evening is not going to be for the faint-hearted.'

'I think perhaps you're right,' Elise agreed as she stood up.

'Your place or mine?' Mark flung an arm around Elise's shoulders and drew her body into his.

'I don't mind,' she said equably, 'as long as it's a permanent arrangement.'

'Hey, Mum!' They heard Angie's voice drfiting on the night as she called after them.

'Keep walking,' Mark urged.

'I can't. Angelique *is* my daughter.' She turned round. 'Yes, darling, what is it?'

'If you and Mark are having an early night,' she grinned cheekily at the pair of them, 'is it all right if I go home with Gary when the party ends?'

'I don't know what you're suggesting,' Elise drew on her dignity. 'You may go home with Gary, but I shall expect you back at the flat by midnight.'

'Sorry, Mark,' Angie apologised with a shrug, 'I did my best, but you know Mum — she's scared I'll turn into a pumpkin if I'm not home by midnight.'

'See you bring Kyle with you, then,' Mark insisted. 'We need to talk to the pair of you.'

'If it's about you two finally getting engaged, it's fine with us. We've already texted the news to our friends.'

'Angelique!' Elise began.

'Better get along, Mum,' she said kindly, 'it's gone ten. Would you like me to get us a pizza on the way home?'

'I don't think . . . ' Elise began.

'I like extra pepperoni,' Mark said, 'with a side order of fries.' He looked down at Elise. 'Sorry, it's a weakness of mine and tonight is a special occasion, wouldn't you say?'

'It's a deal. You can pass on the fries if you like, Mum. Mark, I'm going back inside.' She made to turn back to the party, then quickly twirled back. 'Hey, did you see David dance? Do you mind if he comes back with us later, too? We could turn it into a party. What do you say?'

'So much for our quiet evening in,' Mark murmured in Elise's ear. 'What say we raid the farm shop for extra nibbles?'

'I think Angelique had the best suggestion,' Elise smiled up at Mark.

'What suggestion was that?' Mark asked.

'That you kiss me,' Elise added. 'After all, she has gone back inside as promised.'

'In that case,' Mark responded, 'what are we waiting for?'

As the church clock struck the quarter hour Mark's lips descended on Elise's.

Neither of them saw Angie and Kyle doing a high-five salute on the terrace. They only had eyes for each other.

THE END